喚醒你的英文語感！

Get a Feel for English !

計程車**900**句典

附**2**片錢來運轉 CD

總編審◎王復國
作　者◎Brian Greene

不載老外太離譜

TAXI

計程車費率（日間）

YNM-179

小黃駕駛必備語錄

☑好眼力
☑高EQ
☑900句典

Ｂ 貝塔語言出版
Beta Multimedia Publishing

# 單元說明與使用方法

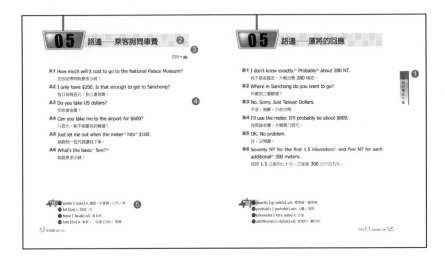

① 側標，顯示目前的頁面屬於書籍的哪個部份。

② 各單元的主題。

③ CD 音軌。

④ 書裡用跨頁的方式來呈現雙人對話，以 A 或 B 區隔人物，每一對話錄一個音軌。

⑤ 隨頁單字。

查詢小撇步：先由 ❶ 側標找到所需用語的分類，再由 ❷ 去搜尋用語的主題，很快就可以找到你所需要的句子。

# 作者序

## 這本書是給誰看的？

　　這本書是為了 (1) 必須用英文跟乘客溝通的中文母語計程車司機； (2) 身在華文地區需要用中文與運將溝通的外國朋友；以及，(3) 旅行到乘客與司機一般都以英文溝通的地方的中文母語觀光客而編寫設計的。學生和英語教師也可以使用這本書！

## 如何使用這本書？

### 如果是計程車司機的話：

(1) 把這本書放在車上。

(2) 拿書給乘客看，指出相關內容。用這本書和乘客溝通的時候，學習說句子。

(3) 開車的時候聽 CD，複誦聽到的內容。

(4) 你代表了你的城市、國家和文化，應該學會做適當介紹。

(5) 複習。

如果是外國朋友的話：

(1) 請你的中文語言學伴、老師或是本地的朋友教你閱讀書裡的句子。

(2) 在空白的地方寫下漢語拼音以記得發音。

(3) 坐車的時候帶這本書，用你日益進步的中文讓司機吃驚。

(4) 複習。

如果是要到說英語的地方觀光的人的話：

(1) 帶著這本書一起去旅行，把書裡的英文句子學起來，以便在國際城市與計程車司機溝通。

(2) 聽 CD，模仿書裡的說法和發音。

(3) 搭計程車時如果遇到溝通障礙，當場就把這本書拿出來。

(4) 複習。

# Author's Introduction

## 為什麼寫這本書？

事實：目前有超過九億的人口說中文。

事實：英語已經變成 21 世紀共通的語言。

答案：很明顯，這本書的立意是把這兩種語言放在一本實用的書裡，以促進東西方的溝通，尤其是針對那些平日就常遭遇跨文化溝通障礙的社會族群：計程車司機和乘客。

## 書裡面有什麼？

這本書是一個溝通工具，充滿了乘坐計程車時經常會使用的英文詞句。書裡不僅包含從載客到抵達目的地一路上所有的必要實用句，也包含了一般的日常生活會話，讓乘客和運將能順利解決問題並瞭解更多有趣的事物。書裡有很多張地圖和圖解，以及與計程車有關的著名電影臺詞，隨附的 CD 希望能幫助讀者改善發音和增進聽力。最重要的一點是，這本書本身就會說話，我們以雙語的排版方式呈現這本書，運將和乘客只需要翻到某個頁面，用指的就能溝通。我希望各位運將大哥們可以用這種方式和乘客溝通，進而慢慢但確實地學習並體驗說英文的樂趣。

## Who is this book for?

This book is for (1) Chinese-speaking TAXI DRIVERS who must communicate with fares in English, (2) FOREIGN FRIENDS in Chinese-speaking areas who need to communicate with cabbies in Chinese, and (3) Chinese-speaking TOURISTS traveling in a place in which the common language between passenger and driver is English. Students and teachers of English can use it too!

## How do you use it?

**TAXI DRIVERS:**

(1) Keep this book in your taxi at all times.

(2) Show it to passengers. Point at things in the book. Learn how to say the phrases as you use this book to communicate with fares.

(3) Listen to the CD as you drive and repeat what you hear.

(4) You are the face of your city, country, and culture. Learn to introduce it.

(5) Review.

### FOREIGN FRIENDS:

(1) Have your language exchange partner, teacher, or local friend coach you on reading the Chinese phrases in this book.

(2) Write Hanyu Pinyin in the space provided to remember how to say them.

(3) Get in cabs with this book and pummel the driver with your growing skills in Chinese.

(4) Repeat.

(1) Take this book on your trip and learn English phrases to communicate with taxi drivers in world cities.

(2) Listen to the CD and learn to mimic what you hear.

(3) Pull the book out in the cab if you experience a communication breakdown.

(4) Review.

## Why this book?

Fact: Over 900 million people currently speak Chinese.

Fact: English has become the lingua franca of the 21st century.

Result: Putting these two languages together in a useful book to allow communication between East and West is the obvious thing to do, especially in a book for those in the trenches of daily, cross-cultural exchange: taxi drivers and fares.

## What's inside?

This book is a communication tool filled with English phrases commonly encountered during a cab ride. Not only does it contain all the usual phrases necessary from picking up the fare to arriving at the destination, it also has the language drivers and fares need to solve problems, make small talk, and learn more about things of interest. There are maps, labeled diagrams, and lines from famous movies involving taxis. The CD is for improving pronunciation and listening comprehension. Most importantly, the book can speak for itself. With its bilingual layout, driver and passenger need only flip to a page and point to be mutually understood. It is through this process of using the book in the cab with passengers that I hope drivers will slowly but surely learn to enjoy speaking English.

Taipei, 2006

# 運將之歌 (by Brian Greene)

CD1 ▸ **02**

I'm a taxi driver
See my cab of gold
I drive around these streets
And that's how we meet

Beep beep beep honk honk beep beep
Burning fuel; the cost ain't cheap

Beep beep beep skid skid beep beep
Arrive in style; leave the driving to me

Beep beep beep crash crash beep beep
We've got to share the road
Driver take me home

You're my precious cargo
Tell me where to go
You feel the city pass
Pavement smooth as glass

Beep beep beep honk honk beep beep
Out where the highways meet

Beep beep beep skid skid beep beep
Hands at ten and two; you talking to me?

Beep beep beep crash crash beep beep
We've got to share the road
Driver take me home

我是個運將
看我這輛金黃色的計程車
我開車穿越大街小巷
我們因此而相遇

嗶、嗶、嗶、叭、叭、嗶、嗶
一直在耗油　油錢不便宜

嗶、嗶、嗶、嘰、嘰、嗶、嗶
瀟灑地抵達　駕駛的事包在我身上

嗶、嗶、嗶、碰、碰、嗶、嗶
我們得共用馬路
運將開車載我回家

您是我最寶貝的貨物
告訴我要去哪
您會覺得好像拿到城市護照
路順的跟玻璃一樣滑

嗶、嗶、嗶、叭、叭、嗶、嗶
一直到高速公路交叉處

嗶、嗶、嗶、磯、磯、嗶、嗶
手往十點鐘和兩點鐘方向轉　你在跟我說話嗎？

嗶、嗶、嗶、碰、碰、嗶、嗶
我們得共用馬路
運將開車載我回家

# Contents

## PART 1 乘客指南——你的救急專區

### Passenger Pages—Point and Go *4*

# PART 2 從叫車到下車

## 2.1 從上車到下車

## 2.2 行進路上（從 **A** 地到 **B** 地）

## **2.3** 從靠近目的地到乘客付錢下車

# *Contents*

# Contents

# 乘客指南——你的救急專區

運將大哥們，還來不及把書裡的句子學到朗朗上口就載到外國客人？還是外國客人的口音太重，你聽不懂？別急，拿出這本書翻到這個部分，讓你的客人用指的告訴你他／她需要什麼服務。如果句子不夠用，可以預先標出書裡其他部分，這樣需要時一翻就到，馬上就能提供乘客更貼心、在地的服務了！

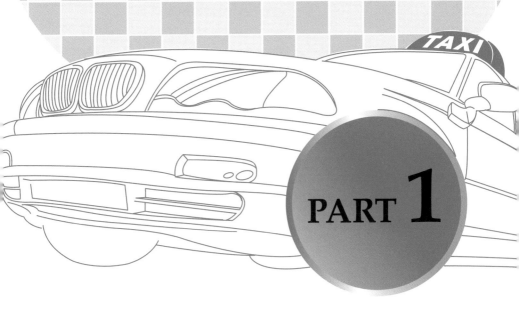

TAXI

PART 1

# Passenger Pages—Point and Go

**Dear Passenger:**

**Use these pages to communicate with your driver. Just point to where you'd like to go—or what you'd like to say—and you'll be on your way.**

## 客人想去的地方

# I want to go to ...
## 我想去……

CD1▸**03**

☐ this address.[1]
　　這個地址。

☐ ＿＿(Aiguo)＿＿ Road / ＿(Tingzohu)＿ Street.
　　＿＿（愛國）＿＿ 路／＿＿（汀洲）＿＿ 街。

☐ the intersection[2] of ＿(Zhongxiao W. Rd.)＿ and ＿(Guanchian Rd.)＿ .
　　＿（忠孝西路）＿ 和 ＿（館前路）＿ 的交叉口。

☐ the ＿(Hongguo)＿ Building.
　　＿＿（宏國）＿＿ 大樓。

☐ the airport / the train station[3] / the closest subway[4] station.
　　機場／火車站／最近的地下鐵車站。

☐ a cheap/good hotel.
　　一間便宜的／好的飯店。

---

**Word list**

❶ address [`ædrɛs]/[ə`drɛs] *n.* 住址；地址

❷ intersection [͵ɪntəˋsɛkʃən] *n.* 道路交叉口；十字路口

❸ station [`steʃən] *n.* 車站；（機構的）站，所；廣播電台

❹ subway [`sʌb͵we] *n.* 【美】地下鐵；（在英國叫做 underground 或 tube）

☐ a good Chinese/Japanese/Korean/Thai/Mexican/vegetarian[5]
restaurant.

一間好的中式／日式／韓式／泰式／墨西哥／素食餐廳。

☐ the convention[6] center.

會議中心。

☐ the World Trade Center.

世貿中心。

☐ a department store / a shopping mall.

一家百貨公司／一家購物中心

☐ the museum / the hospital.

博物館／醫院。

☐ the police station / the British consulate.[7]

警察局／英國領事館。

**Word list** ❺ vegetarian [ˌvɛdʒəˈtɛrɪən] *adj.* 素食的／*n.* 素食者

❻ convention [kənˈvɛnʃən] *n.* 會議；大會

❼ consulate [ˈkɑnsḷɪt] *n.* 領事館

## 02 客人想做的事

# I want to ...
## 我想要······

CD1 ▸ 04

☐ go shopping.
去購物。

☐ go dancing.
去跳舞。

☐ go clubbing.[8]
去夜店。

☐ walk around a night market.
去夜市逛逛。

☐ go hiking in the mountains.
去山區健行。

☐ find a coffee shop[9]/teahouse.[10]
找間咖啡店／茶館。

☐ buy some souvenirs.[11]
買些紀念品。

---

**Word list**

[8] clubbing [ˈklʌbɪŋ] *n.* 上夜店；去夜總會
[9] coffee shop [ˈkɔfɪ ˌʃɑp] *n.* 咖啡店
[10] teahouse [ˈtiˌhaʊs] *n.* 茶館
[11] souvenir [ˈsuvəˌnɪr] *n.* 紀念品

☐ find some really good (but not too expensive)[12] food.

找一些很棒（但不會太貴）的食物。

☐ see the old part of the city.

看這個城市古老的部份。

☐ visit a temple.[13]

參觀一座寺廟。

☐ go to a big supermarket / a bar / a 24-hour restaurant.

去一家大型超市／一間酒吧／一家 24 小時的餐廳。

☐ sing karaoke.[14]

唱卡拉 OK。

☐ have some fun.

找一些樂子。

**Word list**

❶❷ expensive [ɪkˋspɛnsɪv] *adj.* 昂貴的

❶❸ temple [ˋtɛmpl] *n.* 寺廟；教堂

❶❹ karaoke [ˌkærɪˋoki] *n.* 卡拉 OK

# I'm looking for a place to ...

CD1▶05

我在找地方……

☐ buy some souvenirs.
買一些紀念品。

☐ buy some Chinese pastries.[15]
買幾盒中式糕餅。

☐ buy some Chinese/English language books.
買幾本中文／英文書。

☐ buy some cigarettes[16] and beer.
買一些香煙和啤酒。

☐ buy some clothes/CDs/DVDs.
買幾件衣服／幾張 CD／幾片 DVD。

☐ have some coffee/tea.
喝杯咖啡／茶。

☐ sit down and relax[17] for a while.
坐下來休息一下。

---

**Word list**
⑮ pastry [ˋpestrɪ] n. 酥皮點心（如餅、派等）
⑯ cigarette [͵sɪgəˋrɛt] n. 香煙
⑰ relax [rɪˋlæks] v. 休息

☐ get a haircut.[18]

剪個頭髮。

☐ get a drink.

喝杯飲料。

☐ see a movie.

看場電影。

☐ hear some live[19] music.

聽現場音樂。

☐ use the Internet.

上網。

☐ make some copies.

影印。

☐ make a long distance[20] telephone call.

打通長途電話。

**Word list** [18]haircut [`hɛr͵kʌt] *n.* 理髮

[19]live [laɪv] *adj.* 現場表演的；實況播送的

[20]distance [`dɪstəns] *n.* 距離

# I want to eat ...

CD1 ▸ **06**

## 我想（吃）……

☐ some good but inexpensive[21] Chinese food.

一些好吃但不貴的中式食物。

☐ some good Chinese/Japanese/American/Italian[22] food.

一些好吃的中式／日式／美式／義式食物。

☐ some local specialties.[23]

一些本地名產。

☐ some noodles.[24]

一些麵。

☐ Peiking duck.

北京烤鴨。

☐ stinky[25] tofu.

臭豆腐。

---

**Word list**

[21] inexpensive [ˌɪnɪkˋspɛnsɪv] *adj.* 花費不多的

[22] Italian [ɪˋtæljən] *adj.* 義大利（語）的／*n.* 義大利人；義大利語

[23] specialty [ˋspɛʃəltɪ] *n.* 特產；名產

[24] noodles [ˋnudlz] *n.* (通常複數) 麵條

[25] stinky [ˋstɪŋkɪ] *adj.* 臭的

☐ dim sum.[26]

港式飲茶。

☐ hot pot.[27]

火鍋。

☐ somewhere with an English/French[28]/Spanish[29]/German[30] menu.

在有英文／法文／西班牙文／德文菜單的地方（吃東西）。

☐ somewhere famous.

在有名的地方（吃東西）。

☐ somewhere with a view.

有景觀的地方（吃東西）。

☐ somewhere with vegetarian food.

在有賣素食（吃東西）。

☐ really good food.

真正的美食。

**Word list** 26 dim sum [ˌdɪmˋsʌm] *n.* 港式飲茶 （由粵語「點心」音譯英而來）

27 hot pot [ˋhɑtˌpɑt] *n.* 火鍋

28 French [frɛntʃ] *adj.* 法語的；法國的／*n.* 法國人；法語

29 Spanish [ˋspænɪʃ] *adj.* 西班牙（語）的／*n.* 西班牙語；西班牙人

30 German [ˋdʒɝmən] *adj.* 德語的；德國（人）的／*n.* 德語；德國人

## 05 聽客人指示方向

▶ 關於方位，63 頁到 76 頁有更詳盡的說法。

# Basic Driving Directions[31] CD1▶07
## 基本的駕駛方向指示

☐ Turn[32] left. / Turn right.
左轉。／右轉。

☐ Go straight.[33]
直走。

☐ Don't turn.
不要轉彎。

☐ This is the right way.
這條是對的路。

☐ Slow down[34] a little.
開慢一點。

☐ We're almost there.
我們差不多到了。

☐ It's on the left. / It's on the right.
是在左邊。／是在右邊。

☐ This is OK.
這樣開沒錯。

---

**Word list**

**31** directions [dəˋrɛkʃənz] *n.* (複數形) 方向指示；用法說明

**32** turn [tɜn] *v.* 轉彎；轉向

**33** straight [stret] *adv.* 直直地；筆直地

**34** slow down *phr. v.* 減速；(使) 慢下來

☐ Pull over.[35]

開到路邊停車。

☐ Let me off[36] here.

讓我在這裡下車。

☐ Is this the right way?

這條路對嗎？

☐ This isn't the right place.

這不是我要去的地方。

☐ We're going the wrong way.

我們走錯路了。

☐ Turn around.

調頭。

☐ Find a phone. I'll call my friend.

找支電話。我打給我朋友。

**Word list** ㉟ pull over *phr. v.* 開到路邊停下

㊱ let sb. off (at somewhere)　讓某人（在某地方）下車

▶ 如果客人真的很急，第 134 頁有一些句子可以用來安撫客人。

# About Time
## 關於時間

CD1 ▶ 08

☐ My plane leaves at  (10:30 am) .
我的飛機在 （早上十點半） 起飛。

☐ The train/bus leaves at  (5 o'clock) .
火車／巴士在 （五點） 出發。

☐ My meeting starts at  (2:00 pm) .
我的會在 （下午兩點） 開。

☐ I have to be there in  (10)  minutes.
我必須在 (10) 分鐘內到那裡。

☐ Someone is waiting for me.
有人在等我。

☐ I'm not in a hurry. Take your time.
我不急。慢慢開。

☐ Could you drive slower, please?
能不能請你開慢一點？

☐ I'm in a hurry.

我很急。

☐ Could you drive faster, please?

能不能請你開快一點？

☐ Do you know any shortcuts?[37]

你知不知道有什麼近路？

☐ How long will it take to get there?

到那裡要多久？

☐ How much farther[38] is it?

還有多遠？

☐ Is it faster to take surface[39] streets?

開平面道路會不會比較快？

**Word list**
**37** shortcut [`ʃɔrt͵kʌt] *n.* 近路；捷徑
**38** farther [`fɑrðɚ] *adj.* 更遠的（far 的比較級）
**39** surface [`sɝfɪs] *n.* 表面；地面

▶ 第 135 頁有更多相關用句。

# About Comfort⁴⁰
## 關於舒適度

CD1▶09

☐ It's a little hot.
有點熱。

☐ I'm a little cold.
我有點冷。

☐ Can I open/close the window?
我可以開／關窗嗎？

☐ Can you open/close the windows?
你能不能打開／關上車窗？

☐ Can you turn on⁴¹ the AC?⁴²
你能不能開空調？

☐ Can you turn on the heater?⁴³
你能不能開暖氣？

☐ Can you turn on the light?
你能不能打開車內燈？

---

**Word list** ④⓪ comfort [ˋkʌmfət] *n.* 舒適；安逸

④① turn on *phr. v.* 打開（turn off 關上）

④② AC 空調（爲 Air Conditioning [ˋɛr kən͵dɪʃənɪŋ] *n.* 空調）

④③ heater [ˋhitə] *n.* 暖氣機

☐ Can you turn the radio[44] on?
你能不能打開收音機？

☐ Can you turn the radio off?
你能不能關掉收音機？

☐ Can you turn the volume[45] up?[46]
你能不能把音量開大一點？

☐ Can you turn the volume down?
你能不能把音量關小一點？

☐ Can I smoke?
我可以抽煙嗎？

☐ I don't feel well.
我覺得不舒服。

☐ Stop the car. I feel sick.[47]
停車。我想吐。

☐ Take me to the hospital.
載我到醫院。

**Word list** [44] radio [ˋredɪ͵o] *n.* 收音機；無線電

[45] volume [ˋvɑljəm] *n.* （不可數）音量

[46] turn up *phr. v.* 調大、開大（音量或溫度等）（反義為 turn down）

[47] sick [sɪk] *adj.* 想嘔吐的；生病的

## 08 付錢

▶ 第 91 頁到 94 頁有更多找錢的說法。

# About Payment[48]
## 關於車資

CD1▶10

☐ **How much to go to the airport?**
到機場要多少錢？

☐ **How much is it?**
多少錢？

☐ **Do you have change?[49]**
你有零錢嗎？

☐ **Do you take credit cards?**
你收不收信用卡？

☐ **Can I have a receipt?[50]**
可以開張收據給我嗎？

☐ **Keep the change.**
把零錢留著（不用找）。

☐ **One hundred plus[51] fifty is one hundred fifty. (100+50=150)**
一佰加五十等於一佰五。

☐ **Can you give a discount?[52]**
可以打個折嗎？

**Word list**
48 payment [`pemənt] n. 款項；付款
49 change [tʃendʒ] n. (不可數) 零錢
50 receipt [rɪ`sit] n. 收據
51 plus [plʌs] prep. 加上；外加
52 discount [`dɪskaunt] n. 折扣

☐ This isn't the right change.

找的錢數目不對。

☐ I gave you two hundred.

我剛給你兩佰。

☐ You should give me fifty-five.

你應該給我五十五元。

☐ Do you have a calculator?[53]

你有計算機嗎？

☐ Have any smaller bills?[54]

有面額較小的鈔票嗎？

☐ I'm sorry. I don't have any small bills.

很抱歉。我一張小額紙鈔都沒有。

☐ This money is counterfeit.[55]

這錢是假的。

**Word list** [53] calculator [ˋkælkjəˌletɚ] *n.* 計算機

[54] bill [bɪl] *n.* 【美】紙鈔

[55] counterfeit [ˋkaʊntɚˌfɪt] *adj.* 偽造的；假冒的

# 09 英文數字 1~100

CD1►11

| 1 | one [wʌn] | | 11 | eleven [ɪˋlɛvn̩] |
|---|---|---|---|---|
| | | | 12 | twelve [twɛlv] |
| 2 | two [tu] | | 13 | thirteen [ˏθɝˋtin] |
| | | | 14 | fourteen [ˏforˋtin] |
| 3 | three [θri] | | 15 | fifteen [ˏfɪfˋtin] |
| | | | 16 | sixteen [ˏsɪksˋtin] |
| 4 | four [for] | | 17 | seventeen [ˏsɛvn̩ˋtin] |
| | | | 18 | eighteen [ˏeˋtin] |
| 5 | five [faɪv] | 10 ten [tɛn] | 19 | nineteen [ˏnaɪnˋtin] |
| | | | 20 | twenty [ˋtwɛntɪ] |
| 6 | six [sɪks] | | 30 | thirty [ˋθɝtɪ] |
| | | | 40 | forty [ˋfɔrtɪ] |
| 7 | seven [ˋsɛvn̩] | | 50 | fifty [ˋfɪftɪ] |
| | | | 60 | sixty [ˋsɪkstɪ] |
| 8 | eight [et] | | 70 | seventy [ˋsɛvn̩tɪ] |
| | | | 80 | eighty [ˋetɪ] |
| 9 | nine [naɪn] | | 90 | ninety [ˋnaɪntɪ] |
| | | | 100 | hundred [ˋhʌndrəd] |

**補充** 1,000 = one thousand [ˏwʌnˋθauzn̩d]

**Tip** 20 以上到 100 以內的英文數字該怎麼說？

先找出「十整數倍」的英文單字再加上個位數的英文單字，如： 25 為 twenty-five，85 為 eighty-five。

# 10 英文數字 100 以上

CD1 ▸ 12

| 110 | One hundred (and) ten. |
| 215 | Two hundred (and) fifteen. |
| 320 | Three hundred (and) twenty. |
| 425 | Four hundred (and) twenty-five. |
| 530 | Five hundred (and) thirty. |
| 635 | Six hundred (and) thirty-five. |
| 740 | Seven hundred (and) forty. |
| 845 | Eight hundred (and) forty-five. |
| 950 | Nine hundred (and) fifty. |
| 1,000 | One thousand. / A thousand. |
| 1,005 | One thousand (and) five. |
| 2,500 | Two thousand five hundred. |

Tip　上面括弧內的 and 可說可不說。注意！hundred 和 thousand 不加 "s"。

## Basic Driver[56] Phrases[57]
### 運將基本句

CD1▶13

☐ Please look at[58] this book.
請看這本書。

☐ Where to?
到哪裡？

☐ Can you repeat[59] that?
你能不能再說一遍？

☐ Do you know the address / the phone number?
你知道地址／電話號碼嗎？

☐ OK. No problem.
好。沒問題。

☐ It will take about 15 minutes.
大約要 15 分鐘。

☐ Are you hot/cold?
你會熱／冷嗎？

**Word list**
56 driver [`draɪvɚ] *n.* 司機；駕駛
57 phrase [frez] *n.* 詞組；片語
58 look at *phr. v.* 看；快速翻閱
59 repeat [rɪ`pit] *v.* 重說；重複；重做

☐ You can open/close the window.

你可以開／關窗。

☐ Should I turn on the heater/AC?

要不要我開暖氣／冷氣？

☐ Is this the place?

是這個地方嗎？

☐ Here we are.

到了。

☐ Two hundred twenty (220), please.

兩佰二十元，謝謝。

☐ Here's your change.

這是找您的零錢。

☐ Do you need a receipt?

您需要收據嗎？

☐ Thank you very much.

非常感謝。

## 12 乘客常說的一句話

# Basic Passenger[60] Phrases
## 乘客基本句

CD1 ▸ 14

☐ The ___(OneStar)___ Hotel, please.
麻煩到 ___(萬事達)___ 飯店。

☐ I want to go to Din Tai Fung.
我想去鼎泰豐。

☐ Can you take me to a good Chinese restaurant?
你能不能載我到一家好吃的中式餐廳？

☐ How much does it cost to get to[61] the train station?
到火車站要多少錢？

☐ Can you turn down the music, please?
能不能請你把音樂轉小聲一點？

☐ Can you turn up the music, please?
能不能請你把音樂開大聲一點？

☐ Can you open/close the window, please?
能不能請你開／關窗？

☐ Can you turn on the heater, please?
能不能請你開暖氣？

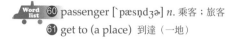

60 passenger [`pæsn̩dʒɚ] n. 乘客；旅客
61 get to (a place) 到達（一地）

☐ Can you turn off the air conditioning, please?

能不能請你關空調？

☐ Are we almost there?

我們快到了嗎？

☐ How much farther is it?

還有多遠？

☐ This isn't the right place.

這不是我要去的地方。

☐ OK. This is it.

好。就是這裡。

☐ Pull over here, please.

請在前面靠邊停車。

☐ How much is it?

多少錢？

☐ Can you give me a receipt?

你能不能給我一張收據？

☐ Thank you very much.

非常感謝。

# 13 英譯中文地址的原則

▶ 用中文地址找路很簡單，但遇上英譯中文地址就可能是難事一樁了！這個單元列出英譯中文地址的常用字，如果真的看不懂客人給的地址，不妨拿書出來對照。

CD1 ▶15

## 中文地址的排列順序（由大範圍到小範圍）：

| 縣／市 | 鄉／鎮／市／區 | 村里／鄰／街／路 | | |
|---|---|---|---|---|
| 段 | 巷／弄 | 號 | 樓 | 室 |

## 英譯中文地址的排列順序（相反！由小範圍到大範圍）：

| Floor[63] [flor] *n.*<br>樓 | Number[64] [ˋnʌmbɚ] *n.*<br>號 | Alley/Lane [ˋælɪ] *n.* / [len] *n.*<br>弄／巷 |
|---|---|---|
| Street[65]/Boulevard[66]/Road[67]<br>[strit] *n.*/ [ˋbulə, vɑrd] *n.*/ [rod] *n.*<br>街／大道／路 | | Section [ˋsɛkʃən] *n.*<br>段 |
| Township/District/City<br>[ˋtaʊnʃɪp] *n.* / [ˋdɪstrɪkt] *n.* / [ˋsɪtɪ] *n.*<br>鄉、鎮／區／市 | | County/City<br>[ˋkaʊntɪ] *n.* / [ˋsɪtɪ] *n.*<br>縣／市 |

**Word list**

63 Floor 縮寫爲 Fl.

64 Number 縮寫爲 No.

65 Street 縮寫爲 St.

66 Boulevard 縮寫爲 Blvd.

67 Road 縮寫爲 Rd.

68 Section 縮寫爲 Sec.

☐ Number 12, Guanchian Rd.

館前路 12 號。

☐ Taipei City, Number 188, Hoping (East/West) Rd.

台北市，和平（東／西）路 188 號。

☐ Songshan District, Number 5, Dunhua (North/South) Rd.

松山區，敦化（北／南）路 5 號。

☐ Taipei County, Yonghe City, Number 668, Yonghe Rd., Sec. 1.

台北縣，永和市，永和路一段 668 號。

☐ Taipei County, Tucheng City, Number 12-3, Alley 55, Lane 342, Tucheng North Rd., Section 3.

台北縣，土城市，土城北路三段 342 巷 55 弄 12 之 3 號。

☐ Wanfang community,[69] please.

麻煩到萬芳社區。

> 上述英譯「街路巷弄」的排列順序依據中華郵政，也常見先 Road/Street 再 Alley, Lane 這種寫法，不管哪種方法，Section 都是跟在 Road/Street 後。

**Word list** ⑥⑨ community [kəˋmjunətɪ] *n.* 社區

# 從叫車到下車

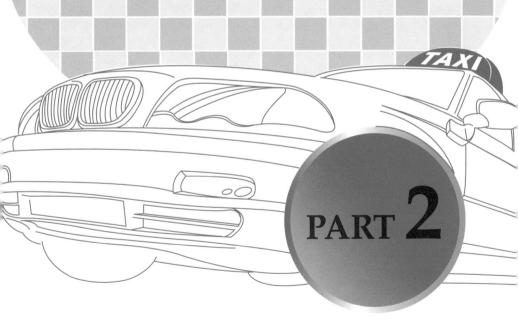

PART **2**

# 2.1 從叫車到上車

這個單元有：

**10** 組運將 vs. 乘客的雙人對話

**3** 種運將在載客時可能遇到的狀況（如聽不懂、不載客、不知道該怎麼走時）

**2** 頁介紹本書的句子

CD1 ▸ 16

**A1** Dad's Cab Company.

老爹計程車行。

**A2** Your location,[2] please?

請問您的位置在哪裡？

**A3** Your destination,[3] please?

請問您的目的地是哪裡？

**A4** Please hold.[4]

請稍候。

**A5** (Someone will be there in) seven minutes. Cab number 187.

七分鐘（會有人去載您）。車號 187。

**A6** Sorry, no cabs are available.[5]

抱歉，現在沒空車。

**Word list**

❶ cab [kæb] *n.* 計程車

❷ location [lo`keʃən] *n.* 位置；所在地

❸ destination [ˌdɛstə`neʃən] *n.* 目的地

❹ hold [hold] *v.* 不要掛電話（等著）；握著；保持

❺ available [ə`veləbl] *adj.* 可取得的；可使用的

# 01 打電話叫車——乘客

**B1** Hi. I need a cab, please.

喂。麻煩你,我需要一輛計程車。

**B2** Taipei. Mucha. Wanfang Community. Number 11, Lane 26, Wanning Street.

台北。木柵。萬芳社區。萬寧街 26 巷 11 號。

**B3** Taipei County. Chonghe. Number 98, Chongcheng Road, Lane 305, Alley 47.

台北縣。中和。中正路 305 巷 47 弄 98 號。

**B4** Thank you.

謝謝。

**B5** Cab number 187? Thanks.

車號 187?謝謝。

**B6** Really? Can you give me the number for another taxi company?

真的嗎?你能不能給我另一家計程車行的號碼?

CD1 ▸ 17

**A1** Where to?

去哪？

**A2** Where can I take you?

我能載你到哪裡？

**A3** Where are you going?

你要去哪？

**A4** Where do you need to go?

你要去哪裡？

**A5** Your destination?

你的目的地是哪裡？

**A6** Tell me where to go.

告訴我去哪。

# 02 路邊──乘客基本句（較隨意）

**B1** The airport.

機場。

**B2** To the Grand Hyatt Hotel.

去君悅大飯店。

**B3** 120 Roosevelt[6] Road, Section 2.

羅斯福路二段 120 號。

**B4** To Veterans[7] General[8] Hospital.

去榮總。

**B5** Taipei Main[9] Station.

台北車站。

**B6** The National Palace[10] Museum.

故宮博物院。

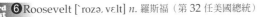

**Word list**
⑥ Roosevelt [`rozə, vɛlt] *n.* 羅斯福（第 32 任美國總統）

⑦ veteran [`vɛtərən] *n.* 退役軍人；老兵

⑧ general [`dʒɛnərəl] *adj.* 總的；一般的

⑨ main [men] *adj.* 主要的；最重要的

⑩ palace [`pælɪs] *n.* 皇宮；宮殿

CD1 ▸ 18

**A1** Hello. Where to?

您好。去哪？

**A2** Good morning. Where can I take you?

早。我能載您到哪裡？

**A3** Good afternoon. Where are you going today?

午安。您今天要上哪？

**A4** Good evening. Where do you need to go?

晚安。您要去哪裡？

**A5** Hi. Your destination, please.

嗨。請告訴我您要去的目的地。

**A6** Welcome aboard.[11] Tell me where you'd like[12] to go.

歡迎搭乘。請告訴我您想去的地方。

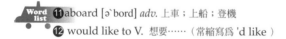

**Word list** ⓫ aboard [əˋbord] *adv.* 上車；上船；登機

⓬ would like to V. 想要……（常縮寫為 'd like）

# 03 路邊──乘客基本句（較有禮貌）

**B1** Hi. Gongguan, please.

嗨。請載我到公館。

**B2** The nearest MRT[13] station, please.

請載我到最近的捷運車站。

**B3** Take me to the Sun Yat-sen Memorial[14] Hall,[15] please.

請載我到國父紀念館。

**B4** Hi there. I'm going to the Cathay[16] United[17] Bank on Sanmin Road.

嗨，你好。我要去三民路上的國泰銀行。

**B5** Hello. I need to go to the Canadian[18] Trade Office.

哈囉。我要去加拿大貿易辦事處。

**B6** Good evening. The intersection of Nanjing East Road and Dunhua North Road, please.

晚安。請載我到南京東路和敦化北路的交叉口。

**Word list**

**⑬** MRT 為 Mass Rapid Transit
[`mæs `ræpɪd `trænsɪt] *n.* 大眾快速運輸的縮寫

**⑭** memorial [mə`morɪəl] *adj.* 紀念的；追悼的

**⑮** hall [hɔl] *n.* 會堂；大廳

**⑯** Cathay [kæ`θe] *n.* 【古】中國

**⑰** united [ju`naɪtɪd] *adj.* 聯合的；團結的

**⑱** Canadian [kə`nedɪən] *adj.* 加拿大的／ *n.* 加拿大人

CD1 ▸ 19

**A1** Hi. Where to?

嗨。去哪？

**A2** Hello, sir.[19] Where can I take you?

先生你好。我能載你到哪裡？

**A3** Good day, ma'am.[20] Where are you going?

日安，小姐。妳要去哪裡？

**A4** Yeah?

上哪？

**A5** Got a place to go?

要去什麼地方？

**A6** Anywhere in mind?

有想去的地方嗎？

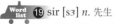

**19** sir [sɜ] *n.* 先生

**20** ma'am [mæm] *n.* 小姐；女士

## 路邊——乘客可能的回應

**B1** Take me here. (hand[21] driver the address)

載我到這裡。（把地址遞給司機）

**B2** Here, my friend will tell you. (hand driver a cell phone)[22]

喏，我朋友會告訴你。（把手機拿給司機）

**B3** I'm going to this place. (hand driver a map[23] and point[24] to a place)

我要去這個地方。（把地圖拿給司機，指向一個地方）

**B4** Go to Nanjing and Chongshan. I'll tell you how to go from there.

到南京和中山交叉口。我再告訴你接著要怎麼走。

**B5** Go that way. (point)

走那條路。（用手指）

**B6** Just get me out of here. / Just go, please. Anywhere! (in a great hurry)

只要把我載離這裡就好。／麻煩開就對了，什麼地方都可以！（非常急）

**B7** First the Zhongxiao-Fuxing MRT station, and then to Mucha. (two people with different destinations)

先到忠孝復興捷運站，再到木柵。（有兩個人，要去不同的地方）

---

**Word list**
㉑ hand [hænd] *v.* 給；傳遞

㉒ cell phone [ˋsɛl ˌfon] *n.* 手機；行動電話（口語時常簡稱為 cell）

㉓ map [mæp] *n.* 地圖

㉔ point [pɔɪnt] *v.* 指；對準

**05** 路邊——乘客詢問車費

CD1▸20

**A1** How much will it cost to go to the National Palace Museum?

去故宮博物院要多少錢？

**A2** I only have $200. Is that enough to get to Sanchong?

我只有兩佰元，到三重夠嗎？

**A3** Do you take US dollars?

你收美金嗎？

**A4** Can you take me to the airport for $600?

六佰元，能不能載我到機場？

**A5** Just let me out when the meter[25] hits[26] $100.

錶跑到一佰元就讓我下車。

**A6** What's the basic[27] fare?[28]

起跳是多少錢？

**Word list**

㉕ meter [`mitɚ] *n.* 儀錶；計量器；公尺／米

㉖ hit [hɪt] *v.* 到達；打

㉗ basic [`besɪk] *adj.* 基本的

㉘ fare [fɛr] *n.* 車資；（交通工具的）票價

**B1** I don't know exactly.[29] Probably[30] about 280 NT.

我不是很確定，大概台幣 280 塊吧。

**B2** Where in Sanchong do you want to go?

你要到三重哪裡？

**B3** No. Sorry. Just Taiwan Dollars.

不收，抱歉。只收台幣。

**B4** I'll use the meter. It'll probably be about $800.

我照錶收費。大概要八佰元。

**B5** OK. No problem.

好，沒問題。

**B6** Seventy NT for the first 1.5 kilometers[31] and five NT for each additional[32] 300 meters.

起程 1.5 公里內七十元，之後每 300 公尺加五元。

**Word list**

**29** exactly [ɪgˋzæktlɪ] *adv.* 精準地；確切地

**30** probably [ˋprɑbəblɪ] *adv.* 大概；或許

**31** kilometer [ˋkɪləˏmitə] *n.* 公里

**32** additional [əˋdɪʃənḷ] *adj.* 添加的；額外的

CD1 ▸ 21

☐ Do you know the address? / Do you have a phone number?

你知道地址嗎？／你有沒有電話號碼？

☐ I need to check the map.

我需要查一下地圖。

☐ I'm going to call the dispatcher.[33]

我要打電話給派車員。

☐ Let me check the GPS.[34]

讓我查一下衛星定位系統。

☐ I need to ask for directions.

我得問一下方向。

☐ I don't know where that is.

我不知道那在哪。

**Word list** [33] dispatcher [dɪˋspætʃɚ] *n.* 車輛調度員；發車員

[34] GPS 為 Global Positioning System [ˋglobl pəˋzɪʃənɪŋ ˋsɪstəm] *n.* 全球衛星定位系統的縮寫

## 07 不載客時

☐ I'm sorry. I'm off duty.[35]
很抱歉，我下班了。

☐ I'm almost out of[36] gas.[37]
我快沒油了。

☐ I'm sorry. I can't go that far.
很抱歉，我不能開那麼遠。

☐ I'm going the other way.
我要走另外一條路。

☐ I already have a fare.[38]
我已經有客人了。

☐ Let me call another cab for you.
我幫你叫另一部車吧。

**Word list**

[35] (sb. is) off duty （某人）不在值班狀態（相反詞「當班」是 on duty）

[36] out of *prep.* 用完；缺少

[37] gas [gæs] *n.* 【美】汽油；瓦斯

[38] fare [fɛr] *n.* （付費乘坐公共運輸的）乘客

CD1 ▸ 23

**A1** Can you open/pop[39] the trunk?[40]

你可以打開後車箱嗎？

**A2** Careful. It's heavy.[41]

小心，很重。

**A3** I'll take this inside[42] the car with me.

我會把這個跟我一起帶到車裡。

**A4** Please keep this side up.

請保持這一面向上。

**A5** Will this fit[43] in the trunk?

這個裝得進後車箱嗎？

**A6** Is the trunk going to close?

後車箱關得起來嗎？

Word list

**39** pop [pɑp] *v.* 砰地一聲打開

**40** trunk [trʌŋk] *n.* 後車箱；大旅行箱

**41** heavy [ˋhɛvɪ] *adj.* 重的

**42** inside [ɪnˋsaɪd] *prep.* 在⋯⋯內部

**43** fit [fɪt] *v.* 裝得下；符合

**08** 路邊——運將幫忙放行李

**B1** Sure. Let me open the trunk.

當然可以。讓我開一下後車箱。

**B2** Let me help you with that.

讓我幫你提那個。

**B3** There's space⁴⁴ inside the car for that.

車裡還有空間放那個。

**B4** Is there anything fragile⁴⁵ in here?

裡面有什麼東西是易碎品嗎？

**B5** Put that in the front seat.⁴⁶

把那個放到前座。

**B6** Sorry. There's no room⁴⁷ in the trunk.

抱歉，後車箱沒有空間了。

**Word list**
44 space [spes] *n.* 空間；空白

45 fragile [`frædʒəl] *adj.* 易碎的；脆弱的

46 front seat [`frʌnt `sit] *n.* 前座

47 room [rum] *n.* (不可數) 空間

# 09 路邊──運將確認位置

**A1** Number 40, Nanjing East Road, Section 3?

南京東路三段 40 號？

**A2** The domestic⁴⁸ airport?

國內機場？

**A3** Is that on Hoping East Road?

那是在和平東路上嗎？

**A4** Chinese Culture University.⁴⁹ The main campus?⁵⁰

中國文化大學。主校區嗎？

**A5** Taiwan University. The main gate?⁵¹

臺灣大學。大門口嗎？

**A6** Zhongxiao-Fuxing MRT station. North or south side of the street? Which exit?⁵²

忠孝復興捷運站。街的北邊還是南邊？哪號出口？

---

**Word list** 48 domestic [də`mɛstɪk] *adj.* 國內的；家庭的

49 university [ˌjunə`vɝsətɪ] *n.* 大學；綜合性大學

50 campus [`kæmpəs] *n.* 校區；校園

51 gate [get] *n.* 大門；出入口

52 exit [`ɛksɪt] *n.* 出口；太平門

**B1** That's right. / No. Number 14, Nanjing East Road, Section 2.

對。／不對,是南京東路二段 14 號。

**B2** Yes, the domestic airport. / No. The international[53] airport.

對,國內機場。／不對,是國際機場。

**B3** Yes, it is. / No. It's the one on Chongshan North Road.

對,沒錯。／不對,是中山北路那個。

**B4** Correct. On Yangmingshan. / No. The one at Jianguo and Hoping, next to[54] Da'an Park.

沒錯,在陽明山上。／不對,是建國跟和平交叉那個,在大安公園旁邊。

**B5** Right. Roosevelt and Xinsheng. / No. The back gate on Xinhai Road.

對。羅斯福跟新生交叉。／不對,是辛亥路上的後門。

**B6** The south side, exit 2 please. / The east side, actually.[55] Drop me off[56] on Fuxing, please.

南邊,二號出口,麻煩你。／是東邊。請讓我在復興下車。

**Word list**
[53] international [ˌɪntɚˋnæʃənl̩] *adj.* 國際的
[54] next to … 緊鄰著……
[55] actually [ˋæktʃuəlɪ] *adv.* 實際上
[56] drop sb. off 讓某人下車

# 10 路邊——無禮的乘客

CD1 ▸25

**A1** Take me to the nearest MRT station. Hurry!

載我到最近的捷運車站。快一點！

**A2** (holding a beer[57] and/or a cigarette) Hey! Taxi!

（拿著一瓶啤酒和／或是一根香煙）喂！計程車！

**A3** Do you understand me?!

你懂不懂我在講什麼？

**A4** Why don't you learn some English?

你為什麼不學一點英文？

**A5** Why aren't you moving?

你怎麼沒在動？

**A6** You can't make me get out![58]

你沒辦法把我趕出去！

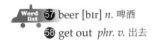

57 beer [bɪr] *n.* 啤酒
58 get out *phr. v.* 出去

# 10 路邊——建議運將的回應

▶ 如果載到這種存心挑釁的外國客人，請別猶豫提高聲量以中文沉穩地回答，或是使用下面這些句子。別慌亂，也別生氣，這會稱了他們的心。

**B1** I'll go as fast as I can.

我會盡可能地快。

**B2** I'm sorry. No drinking or smoking in the cab.

抱歉，車裡禁止喝酒或抽煙。

**B3** Please don't raise[59] your voice.

請不要大呼小叫。

**B4** You're out of line.[60] Show some respect.

你太離譜了。放尊重點。

**B5** Out of the taxi, please.

請下車。

**B6** I'm calling the police.

我要打電話叫警察。

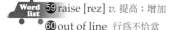

**Word list** 59 raise [rez] v. 提高；增加

60 out of line 行為不恰當

61 respect [rɪˋspɛkt] n. 尊重；尊敬

# 11 路邊──迷路的乘客

CD1 ▸26

**A1** I'm lost.[62]

我迷路了。

**A2** I'm trying to find Jinhe Senior High School.[63]

我在找錦和高中。

**A3** Do you know the Mufa or Meihua hotel? It's across[64] the street from a temple.

你知道「木發」還是「梅花」飯店嗎？就在一座廟對面的街上。

**A4** I think I want to go here. (point at map)

我想我要到這裡。（指著地圖）

**A5** I know how to get there from the big park.

我知道怎麼從大公園到那裡。

**A6** Where I'm going is near the RT Mart.

我要去的地方靠近大潤發。

---

**Word list**

**62** lost [lɔst] *adj.* 迷路的；遺失的

**63** senior high school [ˋsinjə ˋhaɪ ˏskul] *n.* 高中

**64** across [əˋkrɔs] *prep.* 橫越；穿過

## 11 路邊──運將提供協助

**B1** Where are you trying to go?

你想去哪裡？

**B2** The one in Zhonghe?

在中和的那間嗎？

**B3** I think I know where it is. I'll take you.

我想我知道在哪。我載你去。

**B4** Think you can find it on a map? (hand passenger a map)

你覺得你能在地圖上找到那個地方嗎？（把地圖拿給乘客）

**B5** Do you know the way from the MRT station?

你知道從捷運站怎麼走嗎？

**B6** I can take you to RT Mart. There is a bus you can take from there.

我可以載你到大潤發。那裡有一線公車你可以搭。

**CD1 ▸27**

**A1** I need a ride,[65] but I don't have any cash![66]

我要坐車，但是我沒有現金！

**A2** I've just been robbed![67]

我剛才被搶了！

**A3** Someone is following me!

有人在跟我！

**A4** I can't breathe! I'm having a heart attack![68]

我不能呼吸！我心臟病發了！

**A5** (get in cab with injured[69] person) He was in an accident![70]

（帶著傷者上車）他發生意外！

**A6** (get in cab with injured animal) My dog was hit by a car!

（帶著受傷的動物上車）我的狗被車撞到！

---

**Word list**

65 ride [raɪd] *n.* 搭乘；騎乘

66 cash [kæʃ] *n.* (不可數) 現金；錢

67 rob [rɑb] *v.* 搶劫；盜取

68 heart attack [`hɑrt ə͵tæk] *n.* 心臟病發作

69 injured [`ɪndʒəd] *adj.* 受傷的

70 accident [`æksədənt] *n.* 事故；意外事件

## 12 路邊——運將試著安撫

**B1** I'll take you to an ATM.[71] Do you have an ATM card?

我載你去找一台自動提款機。你有提款卡嗎？

**B2** I'll call the police.

我打電話給警察。

**B3** Get in. I'll get you out of here.

上車。我載你離開這裡。

**B4** Stay calm.[72] I'll take you to the hospital.

保持冷靜。我載你到醫院。

**B5** Don't worry. There is a hospital near here.

別擔心。這附近有家醫院。

**B6** Hold on.[73] There's a pet[74] hospital nearby.[75]

別急。這附近有間寵物醫院。

**Word list**

**71** ATM 為 Automatic Teller Machine [ˌɔtəˈmætɪk ˈtɛlə məˌʃin] n. 自動櫃員機的縮寫

**72** calm [kɑm] adj. 鎮靜的；沉著的

**73** hold on phr. v. 撐著；別急

**74** pet [pɛt] n. 寵物

**75** nearby [ˈnɪrˌbaɪ] adv. 在附近

## 13 聽不懂時

▶關於方位，第 63 頁到 76 頁有更詳盡的說法。

☐ Say that again.
再說一次。

☐ Excuse me?
對不起（你說什麼）？

☐ Could you repeat that?
你能不能再說一次？

☐ What was that?
你剛說什麼？

☐ I'm sorry. I didn't catch[76] that.
抱歉，我剛沒聽清楚。

☐ Pardon. More slowly, please.
抱歉，麻煩說慢一點。

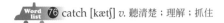 76 catch [kætʃ] v. 聽清楚；理解；抓住

☐ Can you write that down? (hand them pen and paper)

你能不能寫下來？（遞筆和紙給他們）

☐ Can you show me on a map? (get a map)

你能不能用地圖指給我看？（拿地圖）

☐ Maybe this will help. (hand them this book)

或許這會有幫助。（拿這本書給他們）

☐ Can you draw[77] a picture? (hand them pen and paper)

你可不可以畫張圖？（遞筆和紙給他們）

☐ Just tell me how to go.

直接告訴我怎麼走。

☐ Let me get someone to translate.[78] (yell[79] out window, 「小姐，妳會講英文嗎？」)

讓我找個人翻譯。（向窗外大喊：「小姐，妳會講英文嗎？」）

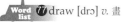

**⑦** draw [drɔ] *v.* 畫

**⑦** translate [træns`let] *v.* 翻譯

**⑦** yell [jɛl] *v.* 大聲叫喊

# 14 介紹本書給外國乘客

▶ 客人上車後如果很無聊，你可以拿這本書給他看。當然，你也可以利用這本書「用指的」溝通或提供協助。最好是將句子學起來，這樣知識帶著走，到哪都不怕。

CD1 ▶ 29

☐ The basic phrases are in the front.
基本句在前面。

☐ Look at the table[80] of contents.[81]
看一下目次。

☐ Look at page[82] 65.
看第 65 頁。

☐ There are some phrases about directions on page 63.
第 63 頁有一些關於方位的句子。

☐ You can see how the fare is calculated[83] on page 42.
你可以在第 42 頁看到費率是怎麼計算的。

☐ Look at Part 3. There are a lot of conversation[84] phrases.
看第三部份。有很多會話句。

**Word list**

80 table [ˋtebl] n. 表；桌子

81 contents [ˋkantɛnts] n. (複數形) 目錄；內容物

82 page [pedʒ] n. 頁

83 calculate [ˋkælkjə‚let] v. 計算

84 conversation [‚kɑnvɚˋseʃən] n. 會話；交談

☐ I use this book to practice[85] my English.

我用這本書練習我的英文。

☐ You can use it to practice your Chinese.

你可以用它來練習你的中文。

☐ It's very useful for taxi drivers.

這本書對計程車司機非常有用。

☐ Go ahead.[86] Ask me anything.

來吧,儘管問我問題。

☐ The writer is really funny.[87]

作者真的很有趣。

☐ Do you want to hear the theme song?[88] It's on the CD.

你想聽主題曲嗎?在 CD 裡面。

**Word list** 85 practice [`præktɪs] *v.* 練習;實行

86 ahead [ə`hɛd] *adv.* 向前;在前

87 funny [`fʌnɪ] *adj.* 有趣的;愛開玩笑的

88 theme song [`θim ˏsɔŋ] *n.* 主題曲

# 2.2 行進路上（從 A 地到 B 地）

開車時要做很多方向的選擇，所以這個單元有：

**2** 組雙人對話 + **30** 句乘客指示

**5** 幅行進方向圖解 + **2** 幅基本方位圖解

**5** 張環境地理位置圖 + **75** 個對應單字

**5** 張地理方位圖解 + **8** 個中英對照單字

**12** 個交通標誌 + **12** 個中英對照涵義

CD1 ▶ 30

**A1** How would you like to go?

你想要怎麼走？

**A2** Keelung Road or the elevated[89] road?

基隆路還是高架道路？

**A3** I can take Xinyi to Jianguo, or take Roosevelt.

我可以走信義到建國，或走羅斯福。

**A4** Is Changan W. Road OK?

長安西路可以嗎？

**A5** Do you want me to take the expressway[90] or surface streets?

你要我走快速道路還是平面道路？

**A6** Are you sure you want to go that way?

你確定你要走那條路嗎？

---

**Word list**  89 elevated [`ɛlə, vetɪd] *adj.* 升高的；提高的

90 expressway [ɪk`sprɛs, we] *n.* 快速道路；高速公路

# 確認駕駛路線──乘客回覆

**沒有意見**

**B1** I don't know. I'll leave it up to you.[91]

我不知道，給你決定。

**B2** Either[92] is fine.

都可以。

**B3** Whichever way is fastest.

只要是最快的路就好。

**有意見**

**B4** Take the elevated road.

走高架道路。

**B5** I think Jianguo is faster.

我覺得建國比較快。

**B6** Go straight to Chongshan North Road, then turn left.

直走到中山北路，然後左轉。

**Word list** [91] sth. is up to sb. 某事由某人決定；某事由某人負責

[92] either [ˋiðɚ] *pron.* （兩者間的）任何一個

CD1 ▸ 31

**turn left**

左轉

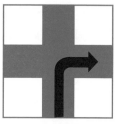

**turn right**

右轉

**go straight to the end**

直走到底

**go straight**

直走

**go around the corner**

繞過轉角

## 基本方位圖解

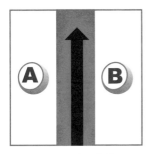

☐ A is on the left.
　A 在左手邊。

☐ B is on the right.
　B 在右手邊。

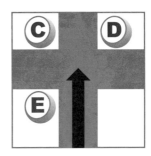

☐ C is at/on the corner.
　C 在轉角。

☐ D is across from E.
　D 在 E 對面的街上。

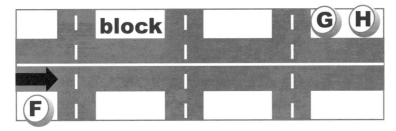

☐ G is two blocks away from F.
　G 在離 F 兩個街區的地方。

☐ H is close to G.
　H 在 G 附近。

CD1 ▶ 33

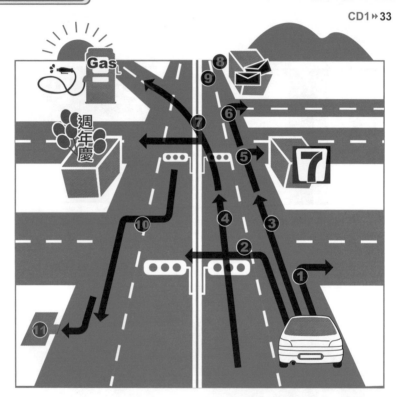

① turn right here  這裡右轉
② turn left here  這裡左轉
③ stay in this lane  留在這條車道
④ keep to the left  靠左邊行駛
⑤ turn right after the 7-11
　　統一超商後右轉

⑥ turn right after the intersection
　　十字路口後右轉
⑦ turn left after 7-11  統一超商後左轉
⑧ right lane  右車道
⑨ left lane  左車道
⑩ change lanes  變換車道
⑪ pull in here  停到這裡

## 04 乘客指示

☐ Stay in this lane.[93]
保持在這條車道上。

☐ Keep to[94] the left/right here.
這裡靠左邊／右邊行駛。

☐ Get in the left/right lane.
開到左車道／右車道。

☐ Slow down a little.
慢一點。

☐ It's coming up.[95]
快到了。

☐ Not this one. The next one.
不是這個。下一個。

**Word list**

[93] lane [len] *n.* 車道；線道；巷

[94] keep on ... 沿……進行

[95] come up *phr. v.* 接近；上來；巷

CD1 ▶35

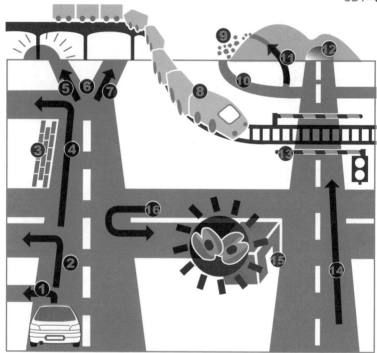

1. 1st left　第一個路口左轉
2. 2nd left　第二個路口左轉
3. curb [kɝb] n. 路邊
4. 3rd left　第三個路口左轉
5. go left　走左邊
6. fork [fɔrk] n. 雙叉口
7. go right　走右邊
8. high speed rail
   [ˈhaɪ ˌspid ˈrel] n. 高鐵
9. landslide [ˈlænd.slaɪd] n. 山崩
10. curve [kɝv] n. 彎道
11. go up the hill　開上山去
12. tunnel [ˈtʌnl] n. 隧道
13. railroad crossing
    [ˈrel.rod ˈkrɔsɪŋ] n. 鐵路平交道
14. go straight　直走
15. betel nut stand
    [ˈbitl ˌnʌt ˈstænd] n. 檳榔攤
16. U-turn [ˈju.tɝn] n. 迴轉

**CD1 ▸ 36**

☐ Turn left/right here.
在這裡左轉／右轉。

☐ Turn left/right at the signal.[96]
號誌燈左轉／右轉。

☐ Turn left/right after the intersection.[97]
十字路口後左轉／右轉。

☐ Take the first left/right after the 7-Eleven.
統一超商後第一個路口左轉／右轉。

☐ Stay toward[98] the left/right at the fork.[99]
繼續往雙叉路左邊／右邊開。

☐ Make a U-turn. / Turn around and go back.
迴轉。／掉頭回去。

**Word list**

[96] signal [`sɪgn̩] *n.* 信號；交通號誌

[97] intersection [ˌɪntɚ`sɛkʃən] *n.* 十字路口；交叉點

[98] toward [tə`wɔrd] *prep.* 向；朝

[99] fork [fɔrk] *n.* 岔路；叉子

**CD1 ▸ 37**

☐ Go straight.

直走。

☐ Keep going.

繼續走。

☐ Don't turn.

不要轉彎。

☐ Stay in this lane.

保持在這條車道上。

☐ This is the right way.

這條路是對的。

☐ Go all the way to the end.[100]

一直走到盡頭。

---

**Word list** 100 end [εnd] *n.* 末端；盡頭

# 07 停靠——乘客指示

CD1 ▸ 38

☐ We're almost there.

我們差不多到了。

☐ It's up ahead on the left/right.

就在左／右前方。

☐ Can you pull up[101] a little farther?

你能不能停前面一點？

☐ This is OK.

這樣可以。

☐ Pull over[102] here.

這裡靠邊停。

☐ Let me off here.

讓我在這下車。

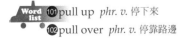

**Word list**
[101] pull up  *phr. v.* 停下來
[102] pull over  *phr. v.* 停靠路邊

Part 2 從叫車到下車

CD1 ▶ 39

☐ I can't turn left/right here. It's a one-way[103] street.

我不能在這裡左轉／右轉。這是單行道。

☐ I'll have to come from the other direction.

我得從另一頭繞。

☐ You can't turn left here until after 7 o'clock.

這裡不能左轉，七點之後才可以。

☐ I can't make a U-turn right here. Let me go up[104] a little further.[105]

我不能在這裡迴轉。讓我再往前開一點。

☐ The road is blocked.[106] I'll have to go around.[107]

這條路封閉了。我得繞一下。

☐ What about when we get to Chonghsiao? Go through[108] the intersection?

我們到忠孝的時候再轉可以嗎？過十字路口？

**Word list**

[103] one-way [ˌwʌnˋwe] *adj.* 單向的；單程的

[104] go up *phr. v.* 往前走；向……延伸

[105] further [ˋfɝðɚ] *adv.* 更遠地

[106] block [blɑk] *v.* 堵住；阻塞；封鎖

[107] go around *phr. v.* 繞；環著走

[108] go through *phr. v.* 穿越；經過

## 09 轉彎進階句──乘客

CD1▶40

☐ Turn left here, but then get in the right lane.

這裡左轉，但左轉後走右車道。

☐ Turn in here, and then go all the way to the end.

在這裡轉進去，然後直走到底。

☐ Go through the intersection, and then pull over to the right.

過十字口，然後靠右邊停車。

☐ Pass  the 7-Eleven and then turn into the alley.

過統一超商，然後轉進巷子裡。

☐ Exit[109] here and then stay to the left.

這裡出去，然後靠左邊開。

☐ Take the second right after the gas station.

加油站之後第二個路口右轉。

Word list 109 exit [`ɛksɪt] v. 出去；離開

CD1 ▸41

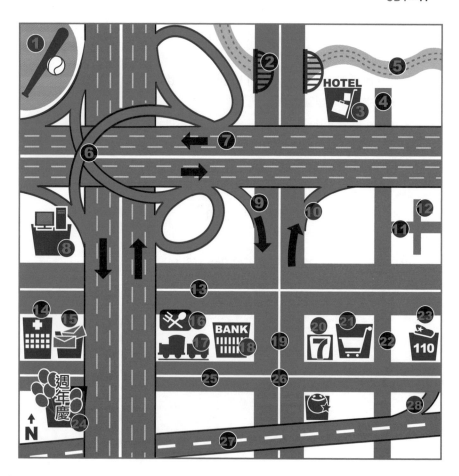

❶ stadium [`stediəm] *n.* 體育場；運動場

❷ bridge [brɪdʒ] *n.* 橋

❸ hotel [ho`tɛl] *n.* 飯店；旅館

❹ dead end [`dɛd ˏɛnd] *n.* 死路

❺ river [`rɪvɚ] *n.* 河流

❻ interchange [`ɪntɚˏtʃendʒ] *n.* 交流道

❼ (elevated) highway [(`ɛləˏvetɪd) `haɪˏwe] *n.* （高架）快速道路

❽ computer market [kəm`pjutɚ ˏmarkɪt] *n.* 電腦賣場

❾ off-ramp/exit [`ɔfˏræmp] / [`ɛksɪt] *n.* （高速公路的）出口閘道／出口

❿ on-ramp/entrance [`anˏræmp] / [`ɛntrəns] *n.* （高速公路的）入口閘道／入口

⓫ lane [len] *n.* 巷子

⓬ alley [`ælɪ] *n.* 小巷；弄

⓭ avenue [`ævəˏnju] *n.* 大道

⓮ hospital [`haspɪtl] *n.* 醫院

⓯ post office [`post ˏɔfɪs] *n.* 郵局

⓰ restaurant [`rɛstərənt] *n.* 餐廳

⓱ train station [`tren ˏsteʃən] *n.* 火車站

⓲ bank [bæŋk] *n.* 銀行

⓳ boulevard [`buləˏvard] *n.* 大道

⓴ convenience store [kən`vinjəns ˏstor] *n.* 便利商店

㉑ supermarket [`supɚˏmarkɪt] *n.* 超市

㉒ street [strit] *n.* 街

㉓ police station [pə`lis ˏsteʃən] *n.* 警察局

㉔ department store [dɪ`partmənt ˏstor] *n.* 百貨公司

㉕ road [rod] *n.* 路

㉖ intersection [ˏɪntɚ`sɛkʃən] *n.* 十字路口

㉗ elevated road [`ɛləˏvetɪd `rod] *n.* 高架路

㉘ ramp [ræmp] *n.* 坡道

地理方位

CD1 ▶ 42

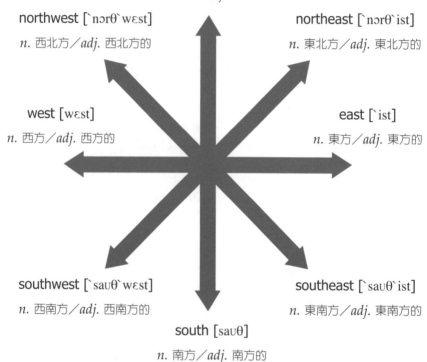

north [nɔrθ]

*n.* 北方／*adj.* 北方的

northwest [`nɔrθ`wɛst]

*n.* 西北方／*adj.* 西北方的

northeast [`nɔrθ`ist]

*n.* 東北方／*adj.* 東北方的

west [wɛst]

*n.* 西方／*adj.* 西方的

east [`ist]

*n.* 東方／*adj.* 東方的

southwest [`sauθ`wɛst]

*n.* 西南方／*adj.* 西南方的

southeast [`sauθ`ist]

*n.* 東南方／*adj.* 東南方的

south [sauθ]

*n.* 南方／*adj.* 南方的

# 12 目的地位置——乘客指示

▶ 參照第 73 頁的地理位置圖。

**CD1 ▶ 43**

☐ The bank is across the street from the 7-Eleven.
銀行在統一超商對面的街上。

☐ The stadium is northwest of the department store.
體育場在百貨公司的西北方。

☐ The computer market is near the interchange.
電腦賣場在交流道附近。

☐ My hotel is next to the river.
我的飯店在河旁邊。

☐ The restaurant is behind[110] the train station.
餐廳在火車站後面。

☐ My office is down the street from the main post office.
我的辦公室就在那條街上，郵政總局再過去。

**Word list** ⑩ behind [bɪ`haɪnd] *prep.* 在……的後面

CD1▸44

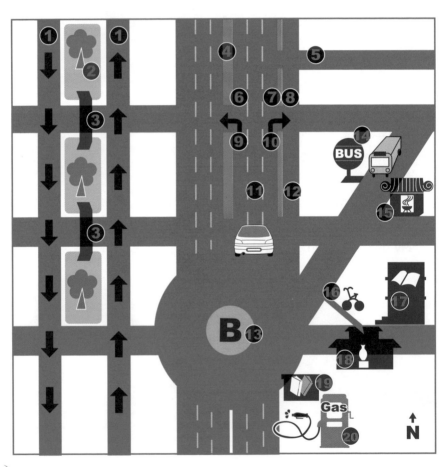

**對應單字**

❶ one way [ˌwʌn ˋwe] *n.* 單行道

❷ park [pɑrk] *n.* 公園

❸ footbridge [ˋfʊtˏbrɪdʒ] *n.* 行人天橋；人行橋

❹ island [ˋaɪlənd] *n.* 安全島

❺ T-intersection [ˋti ˏɪntɚˋsɛkʃən] *n.* T 字路口

❻ inside lane [ˌɪnˋsaɪd ˏlen] *n.* 內車道

❼ outside lane [ˌaʊtˋsaɪd ˏlen] *n.* 外車道

❽ bus lane [ˋbʌs ˏlen] *n.* 公車道

❾ left turn lane [ˋlɛft ˏtɜn ˏlen] n. 左轉道

❿ right turn lane [ˋraɪt ˏtɜn ˏlen] *n.* 右轉道

⓫ fast lane [ˋfæst ˏlen] *n.* 快車道

⓬ slow lane [ˋslo ˏlen] *n.* 慢車道

⓭ traffic circle／roundabout [ˋtræfɪk ˏsɜk!]／[ˋraɪndəˏbaʊt] *n.* 圓環

⓮ bus stop [ˋbʌs ˏstɑp] *n.* 公車站

⓯ temple [ˋtɛmp!] *n.* 寺廟

⓰ bike lane [ˋbaɪk ˏlen] *n.* 自行車道

⓱ library [ˋlaɪˏbrɛrɪ] *n.* 圖書館

⓲ museum [mjuˋzɪəm] *n.* 博物館

⓳ bookstore [ˋbʊkˏstor] *n.* 書店

⓴ gas station [ˋgæs ˏsteʃən] *n.* 加油站

**CD1 ⇥45**

**No Stopping**

禁止停車

**One Way**

單行道

**Slow**

慢行

**No Horn Blowing**

禁鳴喇叭

**Danger/Caution**

危險

**Speed Limit: 60**

最高時速 60 公里

**No Left Turn**

禁止左轉

**No Right Turn**

禁止右轉

**No U-turn**

禁止迴車

**Roundabout**

圓環

**T-intersection**

岔路

## 15 乘客問路／報路

☐ Where are we on this map?
我們在這張地圖的哪裡？

☐ Is this the bridge we just drove over?
這是我們剛才開過的那座橋嗎？

☐ Can you show me where the train station is?
你能不能指火車站在哪給我看？

☐ We're here. (point to origin)[111] I want to go here. (point to location)
我們在這裡。（指著所在的出發地）我想去這裡。（指著某個位置）

☐ Go this way on this street. (point to street)
走這條街的這個方向。（指著街）

☐ Take this on-ramp/off-ramp and go this way. (point direction)
上這個入口閘道／出口閘道，然後走這個方向。（指示方向）

 **111** origin [ˋɔrədʒɪn] *n.* 出發地；起源

# 2.3 從靠近目的地到乘客付錢下車

這個單元有：

**1** 組雙人情境會話，包括靠近目的地時的提醒、車資問題及下車安全叮嚀等。

# 01 靠近目的地——運將提醒

**A1** We're almost there. It's just up ahead.

我們差不多到了。就在前面。

**A2** OK. Here's Muzha and Hsinglong. Which way from here?

好,這裡是木柵和興隆的交叉口。從這裡要走哪條路?

**A3** The MRT station is coming up. Which entrance[112] do you want?

捷運車站快到了。你想到哪個入口?

**A4** Which side of the street do you want me to stop on?

你想要我停在街的哪邊?

**A5** I can drop you up ahead on the right, or go around the corner.

我可以讓你在右前方下車,或在轉彎之後。

**A6** Is here OK?

這裡可以嗎?

**112** entrance [ˋɛntrəns] *n.* 入口;門口

## 01 靠近目的地——乘客回答

**B1** It's just up the street from here.

那個地方就在這條街的前面。

**B2** Turn right at the light, and then make your first left.

號誌燈右轉，然後第一個路口左轉。

**B3** The first one is fine. / The one where the busses are.

第一個好了。／有公車的那一個。

**B4** This side, please. / The other side, please.

這邊，麻煩。／另一邊，麻煩。

**B5** On the right will be good. / Go around the corner, please.

靠右邊就好。／轉彎過去，麻煩你。

**B6** Here is fine, thanks.

這裡可以，謝謝。

CD1 ►48

**A1** You want arrivals[113] or departures?[114] (airport)

你要到入境區還是出境區？（機場）

**A2** Which airline[115] is it? (airport)

是哪家航空公司？（機場）

**A3** Where is your friend supposed to be? (picking up[116] a friend)

你的朋友應該在哪裡？（接一個朋友）

**A4** Where do you want me to drop you? (passengers with different destinations)

你們要我在哪讓你們下車？（數個乘客有不同的目的地）

**A5** It looks like there's an accident up ahead. I don't know how close[117] I can get.

前面看來好像有事故。我不知道我能開多近。

**A6** There's a cop[118] up ahead. I don't know if I can drop you off there.

前面有條子。我不知道是不是能讓你在前面下車。

**113** arrivals [əˋraɪv|z] *n.* (複數形)（機場）入境區；到站處

**114** departures [dɪˋpartʃəz] *n.* (複數形)（機場）出境區；離站處

**115** airline [ˋɛr͵laɪn] *n.* 航空公司

**116** pick up *phr. v.* 接（人）

**117** close [klos] *adj.* 接近的

**118** cop [kɑp] *n.* (口) 警察

## 02　靠近目的地──其他情況，乘客回應

**B1** Arrivals, please. / Departures, please. (airport)

入境區，麻煩。／出境區，麻煩。（機場）

**B2** Cathay Pacific. / China Airlines. / EVA. / Thai. / United. (airport)

國泰。／中華航空。／長榮。／泰航。／聯合。（機場）

**B3** In front of the bank. / Just past[119] the intersection. (picking up a friend)

在銀行前面。／就在過十字路口那裡。（接一個朋友）

**B4** At the footbridge[120] is fine. Then on to Guandu. (passengers with different destinations)

在天橋那裡就可以。然後接著去關渡。（數個乘客有不同的目的地）

**B5** OK. Just get as close as you can.

好。盡量開近一點就好。

**B6** Well, wherever it's safe is OK.

嗯，哪裡安全都好。

**Word list** 119 past [pæst] *prep.* 超過；經過
120 footbridge [ˋfʊt͵brɪdʒ] *n.* 行人天橋；人行橋

**CD1▶49**

**A1** OK. Here we are. Taipei flower market.
好。我們到了。台北花市。

**A2** Do you want me to pull in?[121]
你要我停進去嗎？

**A3** It was nice talking to you.
很高興跟你聊天。

**A4** Don't forget your umbrella/bag/mobile.[122]
別忘了你的雨傘／提袋／手機。

**A5** I just got lucky with the lights.
我剛才過紅綠燈運氣都很好。

**A6** Uh, sir/miss? Wake up,[123] we're here.
呃，先生／小姐？醒醒，我們到了。

---

**Word list** 121 pull in *phr. v.* 停在……；停靠
122 mobile [`mo, baɪl] *n.* 手機 (=cell phone)
123 wake up *phr. v.* 起床；喚醒

# 03 抵達——乘客回應

**B1** This is good. Stop the car here.

這樣就好。把車停在這裡。

**B2** No. This is fine. / Yes. Could you drive in please?

不用，這樣就好。／好。能不能麻煩你開進去？

**B3** Likewise.[124]

我也是。

**B4** Thanks.

謝謝。

**B5** That was fast. Good job.

你開很快。很厲害。

**B6** ... (snoring)[125]

⋯⋯（打呼）

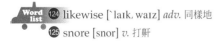

**Word list** [124] likewise [`laɪk,waɪz] *adv.* 同樣地

[125] snore [snor] *v.* 打鼾

**04** 抵達——乘客表示

CD1 ▶**50**

**A1** Wait for me here. I'll be right back.

在這裡等我。我馬上回來。

**A2** There's my friend. She's the one in the red coat.[126] (picking up a friend)

我朋友在那裡。穿紅外套那個。（接一個朋友）

**A3** Can I just sit here a minute?

我可以在車裡坐一下嗎？

**A4** My friend will get out here. Then keep going.

我朋友會在這裡下車。然後繼續開。

**A5** I can't get my seat belt[127] off. It's stuck.[128]

我解不開安全帶。卡住了。

**A6** I can't find my wallet[129]/purse.[130]

我找不到皮夾／錢包。

---

**Word list**

[126] coat [kot] *n.* 外套；大衣

[127] seat belt [`sit ˌbɛlt] *n.* 安全帶

[128] stuck [stʌk] *adj.* 卡住的；困住的

[129] wallet [`wɑlɪt] *n.* 皮夾；錢包

[130] purse [pɝs] *n.* 錢包；（女用）皮包

**B1** I'll wait for you here. / I can't wait here. I'll pull up over there.

我會在這裡等你。／我不能在這裡等。我會停在那裡。

**B2** OK. I see her. （接一個朋友）

好，我看到她了。

**B3** Sure. I'll leave the meter running.

當然可以。我會讓錶繼續跳。

**B4** Got it.

瞭解。

**B5** Let me help you with that.

我來幫你（解開安全帶）。

**B6** Let me turn on the light.

我開一下燈。

**CD1▶51**

**A1** OK. One hundred forty-five NT (NT$145), please.

好。麻煩台幣一佰四十五元 (NT$145)。

**A2** Here's your change—fifty-five dollars.

這是找你的錢——五十五元。

**A3** Your change (is fifty-five NT).

找你的錢（是台幣五十五元）。

**A4** Thank you very much.

非常感謝。

**A5** Here's my card in case[131] you need a taxi.

這是我的名片，如果你需要叫車的話。

**A6** Do you need a receipt?

你需要收據嗎？

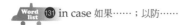

**Word list** ⒀ in case 如果……；以防……

# 05 車資——乘客付錢

**B1** Thank you. Here you go.

謝謝。喏（來，給你）。

**B2** Do you have change for a thousand?

你有錢找一仟塊嗎？

**B3** Keep the change.

錢留著（不用找）。

**B4** You're welcome.

不客氣。

**B5** I'll call you next time if I need a cab.

下次我需要車的時候，會打給你。

**B6** Yes. Could you fill it out,[132] please?

要。能不能麻煩你填一下？

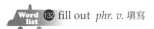 **132** fill out *phr. v.* 填寫

## 06 車資問題——乘客表示

**A1** Two hundred seventy (NT$270)? The meter only says[133] two fifty.

兩佰七十元 (NT$270)？錶上只有兩佰五。

**A2** I'm sorry. I don't have enough cash.

抱歉，我現金不夠。

**A3** I don't have small bills. (hand driver a NT$1,000 note)[134]

我沒有小額紙鈔。（給司機一張仟元大鈔）

**A4** Three hundred sixty (NT$360)? It has never cost that much to get here!

三佰六十元 (NT$360)？到這裡從來沒那麼貴過！

### 乘客後說

**A5** That's OK. It usually costs one hundred ten (NT$110) to get here.

沒關係。到這裡通常要一佰一 (NT$110)。

**A6** Oh, I'm sorry. Here's the other hundred.

噢，抱歉。這是另一張一佰。

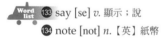

**133** say [se] *v.* 顯示；說

**134** note [not] *n.* 【英】紙幣

**06　車資問題──運將回答**

**B1** There is a twenty NT (NT$20) fee[135] for luggage.

行李有二十元 (NT$20) 的費用。

**B2** Don't worry. We'll find an ATM.

沒關係。我們可以找台自動提款機。

**B3** I'm sorry. I don't have change. I'll get change in that Family Mart.

抱歉，我沒有零錢。我到那間全家找開。

**B4** My bad.[136] I went the wrong way. Just give me three ten (NT$310).

是我不好。我開錯路。給我三佰一就好 (NT$310)。

**運將先說**

**B5** Oh no. I forgot to turn on the meter. I'm sorry.

噢，不會吧。我忘了按錶，抱歉。

**B6** The fare is two hundred twenty (NT$220), but you only gave me one ten (NT$110).

車資是兩佰二 (NT$220)，但你只給我一佰一 (NT$110)。

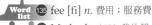 135 fee [fi] *n.* 費用；服務費

136 My bad. （口）我的錯；是我不好。

**CD1 ▶ 53**

**A1** I can't open the door. It's locked.[137]
我打不開門，鎖住了。

**A2** Oops,[138] I forgot to grab[139] my bag.
啊呀，我忘了拿我的包包。

**A3** Could you help me get out of the car?
你能不能幫我一下？我好下車。

**A4** Are you sure this is the right address?
你確定這地址是對的嗎？

乘客後說

**A5** I don't think I can open the door. There's too much traffic.[140]
我想我開不了門。車太多了。

**A6** Maybe I should get out on the other side.
也許我應該從另一邊出去。

Word list
**137** lock [lɑk] *v.* 鎖上；卡住
**138** oops [ups] *int.* (吃驚或是小錯發生時發出的) 哎喲；啊呀
**139** grab [græb] *v.* 抓取
**140** traffic [`træfɪk] *n.* (不可數) 車流量；交通

# 07 下車——運將回答

**B1** Sorry. Let me unlock[141] the door.

抱歉，讓我開一下門鎖。

**B2** Hey, you dropped[142] your keys!

喂，你的鑰匙掉了！

**B3** Let me go around and get the door for you.

我繞過去幫你開門。

**B4** I'll walk you to the door.

我會陪你走到門口。

**運將先說**

**B5** Be careful opening the door. Watch behind you. OK. It's safe to open the door.

開門小心。注意你後面。好，現在開安全。

**B6** Get out on this side. (point)

從這邊出去。（用手指）

**141** unlock [ʌnˋlɑk] *v.* 開……的鎖；開啟

**142** drop [drɑp] *v.* 掉落

# 行進路上

## 3.1 車上閒聊

## 3.2 常見狀況

PART **3**

# 3.1 車上閒聊

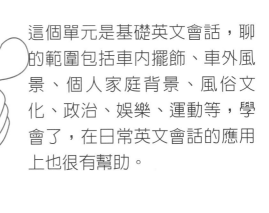

這個單元是基礎英文會話，聊的範圍包括車內擺飾、車外風景、個人家庭背景、風俗文化、政治、娛樂、運動等，學會了，在日常英文會話的應用上也很有幫助。

# 01 車內擺飾──乘客發問

**A1** (point to driver's nameplate)[1] How do you say your name?

（指向司機的名牌）你的名字怎麼唸？

**A2** (point to a picture the driver has) Who's that in the picture?[2]

（指向司機放的一張照片）照片裡的那個是誰？

**A3** (point to charm[3] hanging[4] from rearview mirror)[5] What's that?

（指向吊在車內後視鏡的平安符）那是什麼？

**A4** Can I take one of these? (pull name card from seat pocket)[6]

我能不能拿一張這個？（從椅背置物袋抽出名片）

**A5** What are those? (point to driver's betel nuts)[7]

那些是什麼？（指向司機的檳榔）

**A6** What kind of flowers are those? (point to driver's Yulan magnolias)[8]

那些是什麼花？（指向司機的玉蘭花）

**Word list**

❶ nameplate [`nem,plet] n. 名牌

❷ picture [`pɪktʃɚ] n. 照片；圖片

❸ charm [tʃɑrm] n. 護身符；符咒

❹ hang [hæŋ] v. 吊；掛

❺ rearview mirror [`rɪr,vju `mɪrɚ] n.
車內後視鏡

❻ seat pocket [`sit ,pɑkɪt] n.
前座椅背置物袋

❼ betel nut [`bitl ,nʌt] n. 檳榔

❽ Yulan magnolia [`julæn mæg`noliə] n.
玉蘭花

# 車內擺飾 —— 運將回應

**B1** (slowly say your Chinese name) My name is XXX. My English name is Steve.

（慢慢地唸你的中文名字）我的名字叫 XXX。我的英文名字是史提夫。

**B2** That's my wife[9] and kids.[10]

那是我的老婆跟小孩。

**B3** It's a Buddhist[11] good luck charm.

那是佛教的幸運符。

**B4** Sure can. Call that number if you need a ride.

當然可以。如果你需要坐車的話，就打那支電話。

**B5** These are betel nuts. Want to try one? They're good.

這些叫檳榔。要不要來一顆？它們的味道很好。

**B6** They're Yulanhua. Do you like the smell?[12]

它們是玉蘭花。你喜歡這種味道嗎？

## 02 車外風景——乘客發問

CD2▶02

**A1** What's that over there?

那裡那個是什麼？

**A2** What's that?

那是什麼？

**A3** What's this place called?

這個地方叫什麼？

**A4** Is that a temple?

那是一座廟嗎？

**A5** Is that a protest?[13]

那是集會抗議嗎？

**A6** Does that mountain have a name?

那座山有名字嗎？

**13** protest [`protɛst] *n.* 集會抗議；抗議活動

**B1** See that over there? That's Taipei 101. Have you been there?

看到那裡那個了嗎？那是台北 **101**。你去過那裡嗎？

**B2** Look at that. That's the Danshui River.

看那個。那就是淡水河。

**B3** This is Yonghe.

這裡是永和。

**B4** Yes. That's Lungshan Temple.

對。那是龍山寺。

**B5** That's the Tonghua Night Market.

那是通化夜市。

**B6** That's Yangmingshan. "Shan" means mountain.

那是陽明山。「山」的意思就是山。

# 03 輕鬆閒聊

**運將主動發問**

**A1** Where are you from?

你從哪裡來的？

**A2** Your first time here?

你第一次來這裡嗎？

**A3** What brings you to Taiwan?

你為什麼來台灣？

**運將回答問題**

**A4** I've been driving a cab for about X years now.

我開計程車到現在已經有差不多 X 年了。

**A5** Yes, I am. / No. I'm from Nantou.

對，我是。／不是。我是南投人。

**A6** I've had it for about two weeks/months/years.

我開它到現在差不多兩個禮拜／月／年了。

# 03 輕鬆閒聊

**乘客回答問題**

**B1** I'm from (Canada).

我從（加拿大）來的。

**B2** Yes, it is. / No. I've been here many times. / No. I live here.

對，第一次。／不是。我來過很多次了。／不是。我住在這裡。

**B3** I'm on vacation. / I'm here on business.

我在放假。／我來洽公。

**乘客好奇發問**

**B4** You been driving a taxi long?

你開計程車很久了嗎？

**B5** Are you from Taipei?

你是台北人嗎？

**B6** This car looks brand-new.[14]

這台車看起來像全新的。

 **14** brand-new [`brænd`nju] *adj.* 全新的；嶄新的

**CD2▸04**

☐ Oh, you're from San Francisco. Whereabouts?15

喔，你從舊金山來的。靠近哪裡？

☐ Are you a Giants16 fan?17

你是巨人隊的球迷嗎？

☐ I've been there before. Great Chinese food.

我以前去過那裡。中國菜很好吃。

☐ My sister lives there—Richmond District.

我姊姊／妹妹住在那裡——里奇蒙區。

☐ I love the weather there.

我喜歡那裡的天氣。

☐ My nephew18 goes to school in Berkeley.

我姪子在柏克萊唸書。

**Word list**
15 whereabouts [`hwɛrə,baʊts] *adv.* 在哪裡；靠近什麼地方
16 Giants【美】美國職棒大聯盟舊金山巨人隊（giant [`dʒaɪənt] *n.* 巨人）
17 fan [fæn] *n.* ……迷
18 nephew [`nɛfju] *n.* 姪兒；外甥

# 05 從乘客帶的物品衍生話題

☐ Are you in a band?[19] (passenger has an instrument[20] case)[21]
你在玩樂團嗎？（乘客帶著一只樂器箱）

☐ You must be an artist. (passenger has a large portfolio)[22]
你一定是個藝術家。（乘客提著一只大作品袋）

☐ That's a cute cat. What's its name? (passenger has a cat carrier)[23]
那隻貓很可愛。牠叫什麼名字？（乘客提著一只貓籠）

☐ Busy day shopping? (passenger has many shopping bags)
買了一整天的東西？（乘客提著很多個購物袋）

☐ Must be a special day. (passenger has flowers)
一定是個特別的日子。（乘客帶著花）

☐ Get any good pictures? (passenger has camera)[24]
拍了什麼好看的照片？（乘客帶著相機）

Part
3
行

進

路

上

**Word list**
**19** band [bænd] *n.* 樂團；團體
**20** instrument [ˋɪnstrəmənt] *n.* 樂器；儀器
**21** case [kes] *n.* 箱；盒
**22** portfolio [portˋfolɪˏo] *n.* 手提作品袋；（圖照等）作品集
**23** carrier [ˋkærɪɚ] *n.* 運輸工具
**24** camera [ˋkæmərə] *n.* 相機；攝影機

CD2▶06

運將先問

**A1** Are you married?[25]

你結婚了嗎？

**A2** Do you have any children?[26]

你有沒有小孩？

**A3** What do you do?

你是做什麼的？

**A4** What's your take[27] on Taiwan? You like it here?

你覺得台灣怎樣？你喜歡這裡嗎？

運將回答

**A5** Yes. I was born[28] and raised[29] here. / No. I'm originally[30] from Kaohsiung.

對。我在這裡出生養大。／不是。我原本是高雄人。

**A6** No. I used[31] to be engineer.[32] Now I'm retired.[33]

不是。我以前是工程師，現在退休了。

Word list

[25] married [`mærɪd] *adj.* 已婚的

[26] children [`tʃɪldrən] *n.* 小孩；子女（為 child [tʃaɪld] 的複數）

[27] sb's take on sth. 某人對某事物的意見、看法

[28] born [bɔrn] *adj.* 誕生的（敘述自己或別人的出生，前面的 be 動詞應用過去式）

[29] raise [rez] *v.* 養育；培育

[30] originally [ə`rɪdʒənlɪ] *adv.* 起初；原來

[31] used to be … 以前是……；過去是……

[32] engineer [ˌɛndʒə`nɪr] *n.* 工程師

[33] retired [rɪ`taɪrd] *adj.* 退休的

# 06 聊家庭和個人背景

Part 3 行進路上

**乘客回答**

**B1** No. I'm single.³⁴ / Yes. I've been married about three years.
沒有。我是單身。／結了。我已經結婚差不多三年了。

**B2** Not yet. / I've got two sons and a daughter.
還沒有。／我有兩個兒子和一個女兒。

**B3** I work for the CIA.³⁵ / I'm a consultant.³⁶
我幫美國中情局工作。／我是一個顧問。

**B4** Fascinating³⁷ place. It's got old and new, local³⁸ and international. No place like it.
很棒的地方。融合新舊、本土與國際。沒有其他地方像這裡。

**乘客先問**

**B5** Are you from around here?
你是這附近的人嗎？

**B6** Have you always driven a cab?
你一直都開計程車嗎？

**Word list**

34 single [`sɪŋgl] *adj.* 單身的

35 CIA 為 Central Intelligence Agency [`sɛntrəl ɪn`tɛlədʒəns `edʒənsɪ] *n.*【美】中央情報局的縮寫

36 consultant [kən`sʌltənt] *n.* 顧問

37 fascinating [`fæsn̩.etɪŋ] *adj.* 有趣的

38 local [`lokl̩] *adj.* 本地的；當地的

CD2▸07

☐ The economy[39] is getting better.

經濟漸漸好轉。

☐ Did you hear that XXX is pregnant?[40]

你有沒有聽說 XXX 懷孕了？

☐ The police found the lady who got kidnapped.[41]

警方找到被綁架的那名女子了。

☐ The unemployment[42] rate[43] is dropping.

失業率在下降中。

☐ XXX came to Taiwan to promote[44] his new movie.

XXX 來台灣宣傳他的新電影。

☐ XXX came to Taiwan to promote her new album.[45]

XXX 來台灣宣傳她的新專輯。

☐ There's going to be a grand opening[46] of a new bookstore next week.

下個禮拜有家新書局要盛大開幕。

**Word list**

[39] economy [ɪ`kɑnəmɪ] *n.* 經濟

[40] pregnant [`prɛgnənt] *adj.* 懷孕的

[41] kidnap [`kɪdnæp] *v.* 綁架；誘拐

[42] unemployment [ˌʌnɪm`plɔɪmənt] *n.* 失業

[43] rate [ret] *n.* 率；比例

[44] promote [prə`mot] *v.* 宣傳；促銷

[45] album [`ælbəm] *n.* 專輯；相簿

[46] grand opening [`grænd `opənɪŋ] *n.* 盛大開幕

## 討論時事──負面新聞

CD2▸08

☐ Depression[47] is a big problem.

經濟不景氣是個大問題。

☐ XXX is going to jail[48] (again).

XXX（又）要被關了。

☐ The High Speed Rail[49] Project[50] has some major issues.[51]

高鐵計畫有幾個重大的爭議。

☐ More and more people are using drugs.[52]

愈來愈多人在濫用藥物。

☐ XXX is suing[53] XXX (again).

XXX（又）在告 XXX 了。

☐ The typhoon[54] caused some flooding[55] and landslides.[56]

颱風造成一些淹水和土石崩塌。

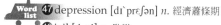

**Word list**

[47] depression [dɪ`prɛʃən] *n.* 經濟蕭條期

[48] jail [dʒel] *n.* 監獄

[49] high speed rail [`haɪ ˌspid `rel] *n.* 高速鐵路

[50] project [`prɑdʒɛkt] *n.* 計畫；方案

[51] issue [`ɪʃju] *n.* 爭論；議題

[52] drug [drʌg] *n.* 毒品；麻醉藥品

[53] sue [su] *v.* 控告

[54] typhoon [taɪ`fun] *n.* 颱風

[55] flooding [`flʌdɪŋ] *n.* (不可數) 淹水；氾濫

[56] landslide [`lændˌslaɪd] *n.* 土石坍塌；山崩

**A1** What do you think about the green/blue party?[57]

你覺得綠色／藍色政黨怎麼樣？

**A2** I read about XXX in the newspaper.

我在報上看到 XXX。

**A3** I heard the government[58] is reforming[59] the retirement[60] system.[61]

我聽說政府在革新退休制度。

**A4** Looks like the green/blue party is having a rough[62] time.

看來綠色／藍色政黨目前處境艱難。

**A5** What's up with XXX?

XXX 是怎麼了？

**A6** Did you see that protest on the news?[63]

你有沒有看新聞報的那個抗議活動？

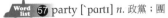

**Word list**

57 party [ˋpɑrtɪ] *n.* 政黨；團

58 government [ˋgʌvənmənt] *n.* 政府

59 reform [rɪˋfɔrm] *v.* 改革

60 retirement [rɪˋtaɪrmənt] *n.* 退休

61 system [ˋsɪstəm] *n.* 制度；機制

62 rough [rʌf] *adj.* (口) 艱難的；難受的

63 news [njuz] *n.* 新聞；報導

## 09 談論政治——運將答腔

**給予正面肯定**

**B1** The green/blue party is doing a good job.

綠色／藍色政黨做得很好。

**B2** XXX really knows what he/she is doing.

XXX 很清楚他／她自己在做什麼。

**B3** I think things are getting better.

我覺得情況愈來愈好。

**予以負面評價**

**B4** The green/blue party is losing support.[64]

綠色／藍色政黨正逐漸失去支持。

**B5** XXX is a moron![65]

XXX 是個低能兒。

**B6** Politics[66] here is a mess.[67] You can't trust anyone.

這裡的政治一團亂。你誰都不能相信。

---

**Word list**

[64] support [sə`port] *n. / v.* 支持；擁護

[65] moron [`morɑn] *n.* 低能兒；蠢貨

[66] politics [`pɑlətɪks] *n.* 政治

[67] mess [mɛs] *n.* 混亂

Part 3 行進路上

CD2▸**10**

**A1** What did he just say?

他剛才說什麼？

**A2** Did you hear that? That's ridiculous.[68]

你聽到了嗎？真是可笑。

**A3** Who/What are they talking about?

他們在講誰／什麼？

**A4** What's the name of this song?

這首歌叫什麼名字？

**A5** Who sings this song?

這首歌是誰唱的？

**A6** What is this ad[69] for?

這個廣告是幹嘛的？

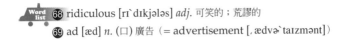

**68** ridiculous [rɪˋdɪkjələs] *adj.* 可笑的；荒謬的

**69** ad [æd] *n.* (口) 廣告（= advertisement [͵ædvəˋtaɪzmənt]）

## 討論廣播內容——運將回答

**B1** It's another scandal.[70]

另一樁醜聞。

**B2** That's the dumbest[71] thing I've ever heard.

那是我聽過最愚蠢的事。

**B3** XXX and XXX. / Politics, trade,[72] finance,[73] health,[74] law,[75] China, art, nonsense,[76] I don't even know.

XXX 跟 XXX。／政治，貿易，金融，保健衛生，法律，中國大陸，美術，胡扯，我根本不知道。

**B4** It's one of my favorites.[77] It's called XXX.

這是我最喜歡的歌曲之一。它叫 XXX。

**B5** This song is by XXX. / I'm not sure who sings this one.

這首歌是 XXX 唱的。／我不確定這首是誰唱的。

**B6** There's a sale[78] at Idee. 25% off.[79]

衣蝶在舉辦拍賣，打七五折。

**70** scandal [`skændl] *n.* 醜聞

**71** dumbest [`dʌmɪst] *adj.* (口) 最愚蠢的（為 dumb 的最高級）

**72** trade [tred] *n.* 貿易

**73** finance [faɪ`næns] *n.* 財政；金融

**74** health [hɛlθ] *n.* 健康；衛生

**75** law [lɔ] *n.* 法律；法規

**76** nonsense [`nɑnsɛns] *n.* (不可數) 鬼扯；胡說

**77** favorite [`fevərɪt] *n.* 最喜歡的東西或人／*adj.* 最喜歡的

**78** sale [sel] *n.* 拍賣；特賣活動

**79** 25% off 打七五折（減掉 25% 的價錢）

Part 3 行進路上

CD2▸**11**

**A1** How much money do you make driving this cab?

你開這部計程車賺多少錢？

**A2** I just bought a new computer.

我剛買了一台新電腦。

**A3** How much do houses cost in Taiwan?

台灣的房價行情多少？

**A4** I'm thinking about buying a house.

我在考慮買一間房子。

**A5** How much do cars cost here?

這裡的車價大約多少？

乘客回答

**A6** It's thirty-two to one (32:1).

三十二比一 (32:1)。

# 11 聊收入和物價

Part 3 行進路上

**運將回答**

**B1** I can take in[80] about one to two thousand (NT$1,000—NT$2000) on a good shift.[81]

好一點的班我可以有一到兩仟（新台幣**1,000—2000**）的收入。

**B2** How much did you pay for it? / How much was it?

你花多少錢買的？／多少錢？

**B3** Near Taipei, around five to eight million[82] NT for about 25 ping.[83]

靠台北的話，**25** 坪左右大概要台幣五百到八百萬。

**B4** If you buy one here, interest[84] rates are pretty low.[85] Three to five percent (3%—5%).

如果你在這裡買一間的話，利率還蠻低的。三到五啪 (**3%—5%**)。

**B5** Used[86] cars are cheap—as low as sixty thousand.

二手車比較便宜——可以低到六萬塊。

**運將先問**

**B6** What's the exchange[87] rate for you?

你們的匯率是多少？

[80] take in *phr. v.* 收進；容納
[81] shift [ʃɪft] *n.* 輪班
[82] million [ˋmɪljən] *n.* 百萬
[83] ping [pɪŋ] *n.* 「坪」，中文英譯（坪為日制計算面積的單位，台灣民間沿用，合約 3.3057 平方公尺）

[84] interest [ˋɪntrɪst] *n.* (不可數) 利息
[85] low [lo] *adj.* 低的；少的
[86] used [juzd] *adj.* 二手的；用過的
[87] exchange [ɪksˋtʃendʒ] *n.* 兌換

CD2▸12

**A1** What are those people doing? (people are burning[88] spirit money)[89]

那些人在做什麼？（看到有人在燒紙錢）

**A2** In English, seven (7) is lucky, and thirteen (13) is unlucky.

英文裡，七 (7) 是吉利，十三 (13) 是不吉利。

**A3** I was born in 1970. I'm a dog.

我在 1970 年出生。我屬狗。

**A4** What's that bad smell?

那是什麼臭味？

**A5** Why are those cars stopped in the middle of the road?

為什麼那些車停在路中間？

**A6** What is that stripper[90] in the glass[91] booth[92] doing?

玻璃亭裡那個脫衣舞孃在做什麼？

---

**Word list**

**88** burn [bɜn] v. 燃燒；著火

**89** spirit money [ˋspɪrɪt ˏmʌnɪ] n. 紙錢

**90** stripper [ˋstrɪpɚ] n. 脫衣舞者

**91** glass [glæs] n. (不可數) 玻璃；玻璃製品

**92** booth [buθ] n. 亭；攤位

# 12 風俗文化——運將回應

**B1** That's called baibai.

那叫做「拜拜」。

**B2** In Chinese, eight (8) is lucky, and four (4) is unlucky.

在中文，八 (8) 是吉利，四 (4) 是不吉利。

**B3** This is the year of the monkey.[93]

今年是猴年。

**B4** That's stinky[94] tofu. Want some? I'll pull over.

那是臭豆腐。要不要來一些？我靠邊停車。

**B5** Probably an accident. When there's an accident, you can't move the cars.

大概發生事故吧。有事故發生的時候，不能隨便移動車子。

**B6** That's a betel nut beauty.[95] She's selling betel nuts. Want some?

那個是檳榔西施。她在賣檳榔。你想吃吃看嗎？

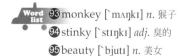

**Word list**

[93] monkey [ˋmʌŋkɪ] *n.* 猴子

[94] stinky [ˋstɪŋkɪ] *adj.* 臭的

[95] beauty [ˋbjutɪ] *n.* 美女

CD2▸13

☐ What's the temperature[96] today?

今天的氣溫幾度？

☐ It's twenty-seven degrees[97] Celsius[98] (27°C).

攝氏二十七度 (27°C)。

☐ There's a nice breeze[99] today.

今天微風吹得很舒服。

☐ What a beautiful day—sunny[100] and clear.[101]

多麼美好的一天──陽光普照，晴空萬里。

☐ The moon is out tonight. Look at the stars.

今天晚上月亮出來了。看那些星星。

☐ It's a nice night tonight, isn't it?

今晚是個美好的夜晚，不是嗎？

**Word list**

96 temperature [ˋtɛmprətʃə] *n.* 氣溫；體溫；溫度

97 degree [dɪˋgri] *n.* 度；度數

98 Celsius [ˋsɛlsɪəs] *adj.* 攝氏的

99 breeze [briz] *n.* 微風

100 sunny [ˋsʌnɪ] *adj.* 陽光充足的

101 clear [klɪr] *adj.* 晴朗的；清澈的

## 14 談論天氣 —— 潮濕陰雨

□ It's really humid[102] today.
今天真的很濕熱。

□ This rain is terrible,[103] isn't it?
這場雨下得很大，不是嗎？

□ It's windy[104]/cloudy[105]/foggy[106]/cold today.
今天風很大／雲很厚／有霧／很冷。

□ A typhoon is coming.
有個颱風要來。

□ What's the weather going to be like tomorrow?
明天的天氣會如何？

□ It looks like it might rain.
看起來像會下雨。

**Word list**
102 humid [`hjumɪd] *adj.* 濕熱的；潮濕的
103 terrible [`tɛrəbl] *adj.* 嚴重的；糟糕的
104 windy [`wɪndɪ] *adj.* 風大的
105 cloudy [`klaʊdɪ] *adj.* 多雲的；天氣陰暗的
106 foggy [`fɑgɪ] *adj.* 多霧的；有霧的

# 15 聊運動和賽事──發問

**A1** Are you a football[107]/soccer[108]/baseball[109]/basketball[110] fan?

你是個橄欖球／足球／棒球／籃球迷嗎？

**A2** Did you see the game?[111] Who won the game last night?

你有沒有看比賽？昨晚比賽誰贏？

**A3** Are you following[112] the World Cup?[113] / Are you watching the World Series?[114]

你有密切在看世足賽嗎？／你有在看世界大賽嗎？

**A4** What time is the game on?[115]

比賽幾點開始？

**A5** Where's a good place to watch the NBA?[116]

哪裡是看 NBA 的好地方？

**A6** Do you play any sports?

你有做任何運動嗎？

---

**Word list**

[107] football [`fʊt͵bɔl] n.【美】橄欖球；【英】足球

[108] soccer [`sɑkɚ] n. 足球

[109] baseball [`bes͵bɔl] n. 棒球

[110] basketball [`bæskɪt͵bɔl] n. 籃球

[111] game [gem] n. 比賽；遊戲

[112] follow [`fɑlo] v. 跟隨；密切注意

[113] the World Cup [ðə `wɝld `kʌp] n. 世界盃足球賽

[114] the World Series [ðə `wɝld `siriz] n.【美】職棒世界大賽（每年十月由美國聯盟和國家聯盟冠軍隊伍出場的季後賽，比七場）

[115] on [ɑn] adj. 在進行的；正在上演的

[116] NBA 為 National Basketball Association [`næʃən `bæskɪt͵bɔl ə͵sosɪ`eʃən] n. 全美籃球協會的縮寫

## 15 聊運動和賽事——回答

**B1** I like to watch baseball. / I don't really follow sports.

我喜歡看棒球。／我其實沒怎麼在注意運動比賽。

**B2** Yeah. It was a great/boring/close[117]/terrible game. / No, I didn't see the game.

有呀。那是場很棒／無聊／很險／很爛的比賽。／沒有，我沒看比賽。

**B3** Yes. I got up at five this morning to watch Brazil.[118] / No. I hate[119] baseball.

有呀。今天早上我五點起床看巴西。／沒有。我討厭棒球。

**B4** It starts at six.

六點開賽。

**B5** There's a good sports bar not far from here.

離這裡不遠有家不錯的運動酒吧。

**B6** I like tennis[120]/badminton[121]/pool[122]/ping-pong[123]/swimming[124]/fishing.[125]

我喜歡網球／羽毛球／撞球／乒乓球／游泳／釣魚。

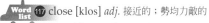

**Word list**

[117] close [klos] *adj.* 接近的；勢均力敵的

[118] Brazil [brə`zɪl] *n.* 巴西

[119] hate [ het ] *v.* 討厭；恨

[120] tennis [`tɛnɪs] *n.* 網球

[121] badminton [`bædmɪntən] *n.* 羽毛球

[122] pool [pul] *n.* 撞球

[123] ping-pong [`pɪŋ͵pɑŋ] *n.* 乒乓球；桌球（=table tennis）

[124] swimming [`swɪmɪŋ] *n.* 游泳

[125] fishing [`fɪʃɪŋ] *n.* 釣魚

Part 3 行進路上

**CD2 ▸ 16**

**A1** So, besides[126] me, have you ever had any famous[127] people in your cab?

那，除了我，你這部車有沒有載過什麼名人？

**A2** What kind of car is this?

這台車是什麼車款？

**A3** This is a nice car. It's roomy[128]—plenty of head[129] and legroom.[130] Smooth[131] ride, too.

這台車很棒。很寬敞──頭和腳的空間很大。開起來也很穩。

**A4** You've tricked[132] this thing out. Custom[133] steering wheel,[134] aftermarket[135] shifter,[136] and a roll bar.[137]

你把這台車改裝了。訂做的方向盤，特製的排檔桿，還加了一組翻車保護桿。

---

**126** besides [bɪˋsaɪdz] *prep.* 除了……

**127** famous [ˋfeməs] *adj.* 出名的

**128** roomy [ˋrumɪ] *adj.* 寬敞的

**129** head 這裡指 headroom [ˋhɛd͵rum] *n.* 頭頂空間

**130** legroom [ˋlɛg͵rum] *n.* 放腳空間

**131** smooth [smuð] *adj.* 平穩的；流暢的

**132** trick out *phr. v.* 裝飾；改裝

**133** custom [ˋkʌstəm] *adj.* 訂製的

**134** steering wheel [ˋstɪrɪŋ ͵hwil] *n.* 方向盤

**135** aftermarket [ˋæftə͵markɪt] *n.* 汽車零配件市場

**136** shifter [ˋʃɪftə] *n.* 排檔桿

**137** roll bar [ˋrol ͵bar] *n.* 翻車保護桿

# 16 哈拉／聊車——運將答

**B1** Ha. Well, one day, XXX got in my taxi. I couldn't believe it! Nice guy/lady.

哈。嗯，有一天 XXX 搭了我的計程車。我覺得難以置信！他／她人很好。

**B2** This is a 2005 Nissan Teana. / You're riding in a 2003 Toyota Camry.

這台是 2005 年的日產天娜。／你現在坐的是 2003 年的豐田佳美。

**B3** It's got the three point two liter[138] V-six (3.2L V6). Plenty of power and good handling.[139]

它的排氣量有 3.2 公升，引擎是 V 型六汽缸（**3.2L V6**）。馬力很大，操控性很好。

**B4** It's not stock.[140] I modified[141] it. Improved the ignition,[142] EFI,[143] exhaust,[144] brakes,[145] and suspension.[146]

這台不是標準配備，我改裝了。點火開關、電子燃料注射系統、排氣管、煞車和懸吊系統都改了。

**Word list** 138 liter [ˋlitɚ] *n.* 公升

139 handling [ˋhændlɪŋ] *n.* （汽車等的）操控性；操作

140 stock [stɑk] adj. 標準的；老套的

141 modify [ˋmɑdə͵faɪ] v. 修改

142 ignition [ɪgˋnɪʃən] *n.* 點火開關

143 EFI 為 Electronic Fuel Injection [ɪ͵lɛkˋtrɑnɪk ˋfjuəl ɪnˋdʒɛkʃən] *n.* 電子燃料注射的縮寫

144 exhaust [ɪgˋzɔst] *n.* 排氣管 (=exhaust pipe [paɪp] )

145 brake [brek] *n.* （常用複數）煞車裝置

146 suspension [səˋspɛnʃən] *n.* 懸吊系統；避震系統

# 3.2 常見狀況

駕駛路上的狀況有千百種,如乘客暈車、車子出狀況、不小心開錯路等,這個單元收錄比較常見的六種。

**CD2▸17**

**A1** Uh-oh. I think I'm out of gas.

喔噢。我想快沒油了。

**A2** You don't look so good. Are you OK?

你看起來不太舒服。你還好吧？

**A3** Hold on! (impact)[147] Are you all right?

抓好！（衝撞）你還好嗎？

**A4** Sorry. I just ran over[148] something. Let me pull over and check it out.

抱歉，我剛才輾到東西。讓我靠邊停車看一下。

**A5** Something is wrong with the car. I have to call a tow truck.[149]

車子怪怪的。我得打電話叫部拖吊車。

**A6** Smells like something is burning. I'm pulling over.

聞起來像有東西在燒。我靠邊停一下。

---

**Word list**

[147] impact [`ɪmpækt] *n.* 碰撞；衝擊

[148] run over *phr. v.* 輾過

[149] tow truck [`to ˌtrʌk] *n.* 拖吊車

**B1** I don't feel well. I'm carsick.[150] Could you pull over please?

我覺得不舒服。我暈車了。能不能麻煩你靠邊停車？

**B2** I'm sorry, I'm going to be sick.

抱歉，我要吐了。

**B3** Look out![151] (impact) My arm[152]/hand[153]/leg[154]/foot[155]/head!

小心！（衝撞）我的手臂／手／腿／腳／頭！

**B4** What's that noise under the car? / What's that smell?

車底那是什麼聲音？／那是什麼味道？

**B5** Hey! Something just fell out of[156] the trunk!

嘿！剛才有東西掉出後車箱。

**B6** Look! Your parking brake[157] is on.

你看！你的手煞車是拉住的。

**Word list**

[150] carsick [ˋkɑr͵sɪk] *adj.* 感覺暈車的

[151] look out *phr. v.* 小心；注意

[152] arm [ɑrm] *n.* 手臂

[153] hand [hænd] *n.* 手

[154] leg [lɛg] *n.* 腿

[155] foot [fʊt] *n.* 腳；足

[156] fall out of ... 掉出……

[157] parking brake [ˋpɑrkɪŋ ͵brek] *n.* 手煞車（=hand brake）

CD2▸18

**A1** Hey! Shouldn't you have[158] turned left back there?

嘿！剛剛那裡你不是應該左轉嗎？

**A2** It looks like we're driving in circles![159]

看起來我們好像在兜圈子。

**A3** You're going the wrong way!

你走錯路了！

**A4** I said to turn left!

我剛才說左轉！

**A5** Could you drive any slower?

你還能開更慢嗎（你能不能開快一點）？

**A6** Why is it taking so long?

為什麼要這麼久？

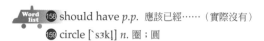
**Word list** ⑱ should have *p.p.* 應該已經……（實際沒有）
⑲ circle [ˋsɝkl̩] *n.* 圈；圓

**B1** Oops. My bad. / Don't worry. This way is faster.

啊呀，是我不好。／別擔心，這條路比較快。

**B2** Don't worry. I know where I'm going.

別擔心。我知道該怎麼走。

**B3** This is a shortcut.

這條是近路。

**B4** Sorry, that was a one-way street.

抱歉，剛才那條是單行道。

**B5** Hold on. There's a traffic camera right here.

別急。這裡有違規照相裝置。

**B6** We're almost there.

差不多到了。

CD2▶19

**A1** I'm going to be late!

我快遲到了！

**A2** My flight leaves at 1:30 p.m.!

我的飛機下午一點半就要起飛了！

**A3** You're driving too fast!

你開太快了！

**A4** You almost hit that dog!

你差點撞到那隻狗！

**A5** We haven't moved in five minutes!

我們有五分鐘都沒動了！

**A6** I'm going to have a baby!

我快生了！

**B1** Just relax. We'll make it.[160]

放輕鬆。我們趕得上的。

**B2** We'll be at the airport by 11:30 a.m. You'll make it!

我們上午十一點半之前會到機場。你趕得上的！

**B3** Take it easy.[161] I'm a professional.[162]

別緊張。我是專業運將。

**B4** Don't worry. Wasn't even close.

別擔心。還差得遠呢。

**B5** Oh, it's always like this at this hour.

噢，這個時段都是這樣的。

**B6** Hang on![163] We're almost at the hospital.

撐著！我們就快到醫院了。

---

**Word list**

160 make it 趕得上；做得到

161 Take it easy. 別緊張；別擔心。

162 professional [prə`fɛʃən]] *n.* 內行人；專業人士（=pro）

163 hang on *phr. v.* （口）撐著；（電話）稍等

CD2▸**20**

**A1** Could you close/open the window?

你能不能關／開窗？

**A2** Could you turn down / turn off the air conditioning?

你能不能把空調關小一點／關掉？

**A3** Could you turn on the heat?

你能不能把暖氣打開？

**A4** Could you turn the music down a bit?

你能不能把音樂關小聲一點？

**A5** Could you turn that up? (radio/CD)

你能不能把那個關掉？（電台／CD）

**A6** Would you mind[164] not smoking?

能不能請你不要抽煙？

turn the volume up

把音量開大一點

turn the volume down

把音量關小一點

turn on the music

開音樂

turn off the music

關音樂

**Word list** 164 mind + V-ing 介意……

# 04 舒適度──運將回應

**B1** Certainly.[165]

當然可以。

**B2** Yes, sir. / Yes, ma'am.

好的，先生。／好的，小姐。

**B3** No problem.[166]

沒問題。

**B4** Sure.

當然（好）。

**B5** How's this? (ask about the volume level)[167]

這樣可以嗎？（詢問音量大小）

**B6** I'm sorry. (put out[168] cigarette)

抱歉。（把香煙捻熄）

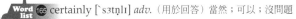

**Word list**

[165] certainly [`sɝtṇlɪ] *adv.* （用於回答）當然；可以；沒問題

[166] No problem. （回應要求）沒問題；（回應別人的道謝或道歉）哪裡，沒關係

[167] volume level [`vɑljəm ˌlɛvl] *n.* 音量大小

[168] put out *phr. v.* 熄滅；關掉

CD2►21

☐ **That guy just cut me off!**[167]

那傢伙剛剛插到我前面。

☐ **Why won't this guy let me in?**[168]

為什麼這個傢伙不讓我插進去？

☐ **What's this idiot**[169] **doing?**

這個白痴在做什麼？

☐ **Passing like that is dangerous.**

那樣超（過）很危險。

☐ **That guy is driving like a maniac!**[170]

那傢伙開車像瘋子一樣。

☐ **Whoa! That was close!**

哇！好危險！

**Word list**
[167] cut off *phr. v.* 切斷；打斷
[168] let in *phr. v.* 讓⋯⋯進來
[169] idiot [ˋɪdɪət] *n.* 白痴；笨蛋
[170] maniac [ˋmenɪˏæk] *n.* （口）瘋子

## 遇見事故發生

CD2▸22

☐ It looks like a fender-bender[171] up ahead.

看來前面好像有小擦撞。

☐ That car is totaled.[172]

那台車報廢了。

☐ It was a head-on[173] collision.[174]

那個是正面對撞。

☐ The driver lost control and ran into a tree.

那個駕駛失控撞上一棵樹。

☐ The car spun out[175] and got hit by a bus.

那台車打滑出去，被一輛巴士撞到。

☐ I swerved[176] to miss[177] the dog and sideswiped[178] a wall.

我快速閃避為了避開那隻狗，卻擦牆。

**Word list**
171. fender-bender [`fɛndɚ, bɛndɚ] *n.* 小車禍；擦撞
172. total [`totl] *v.* （口）徹底摧毀
173. head-on [`hɛd`ɑn] *adj.* 迎面的；正面的
174. collision [kə`lɪʒən] *n.* 碰撞；相撞
175. spin [spɪn] *v.* 旋轉
176. swerve [swɝv] *v.* 偏離方向；突然轉向
177. miss [mɪs] *v.* 避開；躲過；漏掉
178. sideswipe [`saɪd, swaɪp] *v.* 沿邊擦過

# 英文加油站

**4.1** 計程車相關各類圖表

**4.2** 運將休息站

PART **4**

# 4.1 計程車相關各類圖表

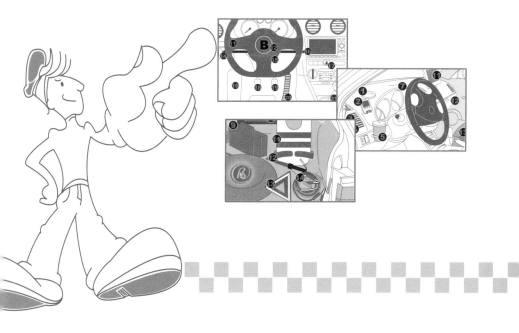

CD2▸23

> **TAXI FARE (Daytime)**[1]
> **6:00 a.m. to 11:00 p.m.**
> **within 1.5 km: NT$70**
> **over 1.5 km: NT$5 per 300 m**
> **waiting: NT$5 per 2 minutes**

There is a NT$ 20 surcharge[2] for taxi fares after 11 p.m.

DRIVER CARRIES ONLY NT$150 CHANGE

Four Passengers Maximum[3]

Flat[4] Rate NT$1,000 to Airport

**Word list**

❶ daytime [ˋde͵taɪm] *n.* 白天
❷ surcharge [ˋsɝ͵tʃɑrdʒ] *n.* 額外費用
❸ maximum [ˋmæksəməm] *n.* 最大量；最高額度
❹ flat [flæt] *adj.* 均一的；一律的

計程車費率（日間）

凌晨六點到夜間十一點

**1.5** 公里內：台幣 **70** 元

**1.5** 公里以上：每 **300** 公尺台幣 **5**元

延滯計時：每 **2** 分鐘台幣 **5**元

夜間十一點之後計程車資每一旅次加收台幣 **20** 元

司機只有台幣 **150** 元的零錢可以找

最大載客量：四人

到機場單一費率：台幣 **1,000** 元

CD2▶24

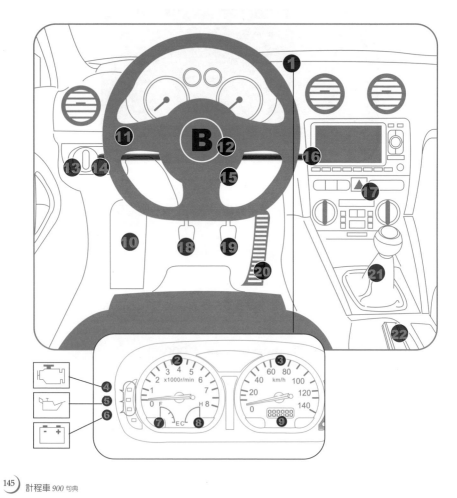

❶ dashboard [ˋdæʃˌbɔrd] *n.* 儀錶板

❷ tachometer [təˋkɑmətɚ] *n.*
引擎轉速表

❸ speedometer [spiˋdɑmətɚ] *n.*
時速表；速率表

❹ check engine light
[ˋtʃɛk ˋɛndʒən ˌlaɪt] *n.*
引擎故障警示燈

❺ oil pressure gauge
[ˋɔɪl ˌprɛʃɚ ˌgedʒ] *n.* 油壓表

❻ battery indicator
[ˋbætərɪ ˋɪndəˌketɚ] *n.* 電量指示表

❼ gas gauge [ˋgæs ˌgedʒ] *n.* 油量表

❽ temperature gauge
[ˋtɛmpərətʃɚ ˌgedʒ] *n.* 溫度表

❾ odometer [oˋdɑmətɚ] *n.* 里程表

❿ controls [kənˋtrolz] *n.* (複數形)
操縱裝置

⓫ steering wheel [ˋstɪrɪŋ ˌhwil] *n.*
方向盤

⓬ horn [hɔrn] *n.* 喇叭

⓭ headlight switch [ˋhɛdˌlaɪt ˌswɪtʃ] *n.*
頭燈開關

⓮ windshield wiper switch
[ˋwɪndˌʃild ˌwaɪpɚ ˌswɪtʃ] *n.* 雨刷開關

⓯ ignition switch [ɪgˋnɪʃən ˌswɪtʃ] *n.*
電門；點火開關

⓰ turn signal switch
[ˋtɜn ˌsɪgnḷ ˌswɪtʃ] *n.* 方向燈開關

⓱ hazard light switch
[ˋhæzɚd ˌlaɪt ˌswɪtʃ] *n.* 危險警告燈開關

⓲ clutch (pedal) [ˋklʌtʃ (ˌpɛdḷ) ] *n.*
離合器（踏板）

⓳ brake (pedal) [ˋbrek (ˌpɛdḷ) ] *n.*
煞車（踏板）；腳煞車

⓴ gas (pedal) / accelerator
[ˋgæs (ˌpɛdḷ) ] / [ækˋsɛləˌretɚ] *n.* 油門

㉑ gear shift / stick (shift)
[ˋgɪr ˌʃift] / [ˋstɪk (ˌʃift ) ] *n.* 排檔桿

㉒ emergency brake / parking brake
[ɪˋmɝdʒənsɪ ˌbrek] / [ˋpɑrkɪŋ ˌbrek] *n.*
手煞車

CD2 ▶ 25

☐ I step[5] on the brake (pedal) to slow down and stop.
我踩煞車（踏板）來減速停車。

☐ I turn the steering wheel to turn and go around corners.
我轉動方向盤以轉過街角。

☐ I use the gearshift and clutch to upshift[6] and downshift.[7]
我用排檔桿跟離合器來轉換高低檔。

☐ I step on the gas (pedal) to accelerate.[8]
我踩油門（踏板）來加速。

☐ I turn the key in the ignition switch to start the engine.
我轉動插在電門裡的鑰匙來啟動引擎。

☐ The speedometer tells me how fast the car is going.
時速表告訴我車子目前跑多快。

**Word list**
⑤ step [stɛp] v. 踩；踏
⑥ upshift [`ʌp͵ʃɪft] v. 換到高檔
⑦ downshift [`daʊn͵ʃɪft] v. 換到低檔
⑧ accelerate [æk`sɛlə͵ret] v. （使⋯⋯）加速

CD2▸26

☐ My son stepped on the gas instead of⁹ the brake. That's why the front bumper¹⁰ looks like that.

我兒子錯把油門當煞車踩。那就是為什麼前保險桿看起來是那副德性的原因。

☐ The steering wheel locks automatically¹¹ when I take the key out of the ignition.

在我把鑰匙拔出電門時，方向盤就會自動上鎖。

☐ Why do you have a skull¹² on your gearshift?

你為什麼要在排檔桿上套骷髏頭？

☐ It's getting pretty dark. Shouldn't you turn your headlights on?

天色變得非常暗。你不是應該把頭燈打開嗎？

☐ What's that red light that keeps flashing?¹³ It isn't the check engine light, is it?

那個一直在閃的紅燈是什麼？那不會是引擎故障警示燈吧，是嗎？

☐ The speedometer broke¹⁴ a few weeks ago. Now I just go by¹⁵ feeling.

時速表幾個禮拜前壞了。現在我憑感覺開車。

**Word list**

⑨ A instead of B 是 A 而不是 B；A 取代 B

⑩ bumper [`bʌmpɚ] n. （汽車）保險桿

⑪ automatically [ˌɔtə`mætɪk‖ɪ] adv. 自動地；機械地

⑫ skull [skʌl] n. 骷髏頭；頭骨

⑬ flash [flæʃ] v. 閃爍；掠過

⑭ break [brek] v. 損壞；破裂

⑮ go by (sth.) 憑（某事物）判斷

Part 4 英文加油站

CD2▸27

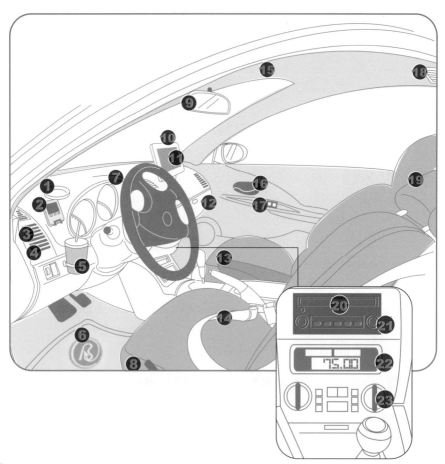

❶ ashtray [`æʃˌtre] *n.* 煙灰缸

❷ global positioning system [ `globl pə`zɪʃənɪŋ ˌsɪstəm] *n.*
全球衛星定位系統（常簡稱 GPS）

❸ heater [`hitɚ] *n.* 暖氣

❹ air conditioning [`ɛr kənˌdɪʃənɪŋ] *n.* 空調系統（常簡稱 AC）

❺ drink holder [`drɪŋk ˌholdɚ] *n.* 飲料架

❻ floor mat [`flor ˌmæt] *n.* 腳踏墊

❼ dash [dæʃ] *n.*（口）儀錶板 (=dashboard)

❽ seat adjustment lever [`sit ə`dʒʌstmənt ˌlɛvɚ] *n.* 椅背調整桿

❾ rearview mirror [`rɪrˌvju `mɪrɚ] *n.* 車內後視鏡

❿ KTV machine [`ke `ti `vi məˌʃɪŋ] *n.* 卡拉 OK 伴唱機

⓫ video screen [`vɪdɪˌoˌskrin] *n.* 銀幕畫面

⓬ glove box / glove compartment
[`glʌvˌbɑks]/[`glʌv kəmˌpɑrtmənt] *n.* 前座置物箱

接下頁

承前頁

⓭ armrest [`ɑrmˌrɛst] *n.* 扶手

⓮ seat belt / safety belt [`sit ˌbɛlt] / [`sefti ˌbɛlt] *n.*
安全帶

⓯ headliner [`hɛdˌlaɪnə] *n.* 車頂內飾布

⓰ door handle [`dor ˌhændl] *n.* 門把

⓱ window control / window switch
[`wɪndo kənˌtrol] / [`wɪndo ˌswɪtʃ] *n.* 窗戶開關

⓲ cabin light [`kæbɪn ˌlaɪt] *n.* 車頂室內燈；座艙閱讀燈

⓳ headrest [`hɛdˌrɛst] *n.* 靠頭枕

⓴ radio [`redɪˌo] *n.* 電台；收音機；無線電

㉑ volume knob [`vɑljəm ˌnɑb] *n.* 音量鈕

㉒ meter [`mitə] *n.* 計費錶

㉓ climate controls [`klaɪmɪt kənˌtrolz] *n.* (複數形)
氣溫控制裝置；冷暖空調設備

### 03 例句

☐ You can move the seat back if you want. Just pull the lever on the side.

如果你想要的話，可以把座椅往後調。只要拉旁邊的桿子就可以了。

☐ Please put on[16]/fasten[17] your seatbelt.

請繫上你的安全帶。

☐ Let me turn down the AC.

讓我把空調關小一點。

☐ I can turn up the heater if you're cold.

如果你會冷的話，我可以把暖氣開大一點。

☐ The ashtray is between the seats.

煙灰缸在座位之間。

☐ The window control is on the armrest.

窗戶開關在扶手上。

Part 4 英文加油站

---

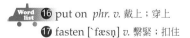 **Word list** ⓰ put on *phr. v.* 戴上；穿上

　　　　⓱ fasten [`fæsn] *v.* 繫緊；扣住

CD2▸29

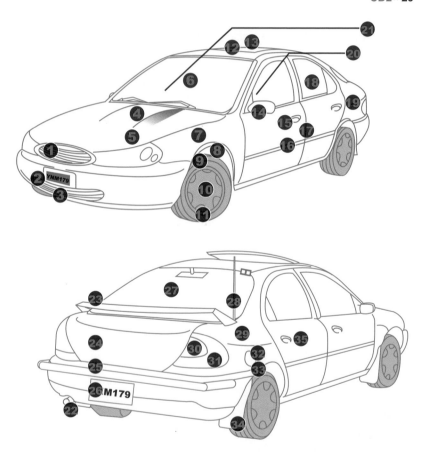

❶ grille [grɪl] *n.* 水箱護罩

❷ air dam [ˋɛr ˏdæm] *n.*
前進氣壩；前下巴

❸ air vent / intake
[ˋɛr ˏvɛnt] / [ˋɪn ˏtek] *n.* 進氣孔

❹ body contour [ˋbɑdɪ ˏkɑntʊr] *n.*
車身輪廓；車型線條

❺ hood [hʊd] *n.* 引擎蓋

❻ windshield [ˋwɪnd ˏʃild] *n.*
擋風玻璃

❼ front fender [ˋfrʌnt ˋfɛndɚ] *n.*
前葉子板

❽ wheel opening [ˋhwil ˏopənɪŋ] *n.*
輪拱

❾ tire [taɪr] *n.* 輪胎

❿ wheel [hwil] *n.* 輪圈

⓫ disc brake [ˋdɪsk ˏbrek] *n.* 碟煞

⓬ roof [ruf] *n.* 車頂

⓭ sun roof [ˋsʌn ˏruf] *n.* 天窗

⓮ sideview mirror
[ˋsaɪd ˏvju ˋmɪrɚ] *n.* 後視鏡

⓯ door handle [ˋdor ˏhændl̩] *n.* 門把

⓰ trim [trɪm] *n.* 車側飾條

⓱ door seam [ˋdor ˏsim] *n.* 車門縫隙

⓲ rear-side window
[ˋrɪr ˏsaɪd ˋwɪndo] *n.* 後座側窗

⓳ rear fender [ˋrɪr ˋfɛndɚ] *n.* 後葉子板

⓴ driver side [ˋdraɪvɚ ˏsaɪd] *n.* 駕駛側

㉑ passenger side [ˋpæsn̩dʒɚ ˏsaɪd] *n.*
前座乘客側

㉒ exhaust (pipe) / tailpipe
[ɪgˋzɔst (ˏpaɪp)] / [ˋtel ˏpaɪp] *n.*
排氣管；尾管

㉓ spoiler [ˋspɔɪlɚ] *n.* 尾翼；擾流翼

㉔ trunk [trʌŋk] *n.* 後車箱

㉕ bumper [ˋbʌmpɚ] *n.* 保險桿；防撞桿

㉖ license plate [ˋlaɪsn̩s ˏplet] *n.* 車牌

㉗ rear window [ˋrɪr ˋwɪndo] *n.* 車尾窗

㉘ antenna [ænˋtɛnə] *n.* 天線

㉙ body panel [ˋbɑdɪ ˏpænl̩] *n.* 車身鈑件

㉚ reverse light [rɪˋvɝs ˏlaɪt] *n.* 倒車燈

㉛ tail light [ˋtel ˏlaɪt] *n.* 尾燈

㉜ gas cap [ˋgæs ˏkæp] *n.* 油箱蓋

㉝ fuel door [ˋfjuəl ˏdor] *n.* 油箱外蓋

㉞ mudguard [ˋmʌd ˏgɑrd] *n.* 擋泥板

㉟ door [dor] *n.* 車門

CD2 ▸ **30**

❶ windshield wiper [`wɪnd͵ʃild ͵waɪpɚ] *n.* 擋風玻璃雨刷

❷ windshield washer fluid bottle

　　[`wɪnd͵ʃild ͵wɑʃɚ `fluɪd ͵bɑtl] *n.* 雨刷水箱

❸ radiator overflow tank

　　[`redɪ͵etɚ `ovɚ͵flo ͵tæŋk] *n.* 副水箱

❹ automatic transmission

　　[͵ɔtə`mætɪk træns`mɪʃən] *n.* 自動變速器（常簡稱 AT）

❺ automatic transmission fluid filler

　　[͵ɔtə`mætɪk træns`mɪʃən `fluɪd ͵fɪlɚ] *n.* 自動變速器油口

❻ ATF dipstick [`e `ti `ɛf `dɪp͵stɪk] *n.* 自動變速器油尺

❼ radiator hose [`redɪ͵etɚ ͵hoz] *n.* 水管

❽ dipstick [`dɪp͵stɪk] *n.* 油尺

❾ alternator [`ɔltɚ͵netɚ] *n.* 交流發電機

❿ radiator [`redɪ͵etɚ] *n.* 水箱；汽車散熱器

⓫ grille [`grɪl] *n.* 水箱護罩

接下頁

承前頁

**⑫** spark plug [ˋspɑrk ˌplʌg] *n.* 火星塞

**⑬** spark plug wire [ˋspɑrk ˌplʌg ˌwaɪr] *n.* 火星塞線

**⑭** valve cover [ˋvælv ˌkʌvɚ] *n.* 汽缸蓋

**⑮** oil filler cap [ˋɔɪl ˌfɪlɚ ˌkæp] *n.* 機油蓋

**⑯** hood latch [ˋhʊd ˌlætʃ] *n.* 引擎蓋鎖閂

**⑰** air cleaner [ˋɛr ˌklinɚ] *n.* 空氣濾清器

**⑱** battery [ˋbætərɪ] *n.* 電瓶

**⑲** fuse panel [ˋfjuz ˌpænl] *n.* 保險絲座

**⑳** headlight [ˋhɛdˌlaɪt] *n.* 頭燈

**㉑** turn signal (indicator) [ˋtɜn ˌsɪgŋl (ˋɪndəˌketɚ)] *n.* 方向燈

**㉒** power steering pump
[ˋpaʊɚ ˋstɪrɪŋ ˌpʌmp] *n.* 動力液壓幫浦

☐ I need to add some power steering fluid to the power steering pump.

我需要在動力液壓幫浦加一些動力方向機油。

☐ The battery is dead.[18] I need a jump.[19] Maybe the alternator is bad.

電瓶掛了。我需要接電發車。交流發電機可能壞了。

☐ The radiator (hose) is leaking.[20]

水箱（的水管）在漏水。

☐ The windshield washer fluid bottle is empty.[21]

雨刷水箱是空的。

☐ I need to check the oil.[22] Where is the dipstick?

我得檢查一下機油。油尺在哪裡？

☐ There is an oil leak from the valve cover.

汽缸蓋有地方在漏油。

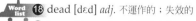

**18** dead [dɛd] *adj.* 不運作的；失效的

**19** jump [dʒʌmp] *n.* 接電發車 (=jump start [`dʒʌmp ˌstɑrt] *n.*)

**20** leak [lik] *v.* 漏；滲

**21** empty [`ɛmptɪ] *adj.* 空的

**22** oil [ɔɪl] *n.* 機油；石油

CD2▸32

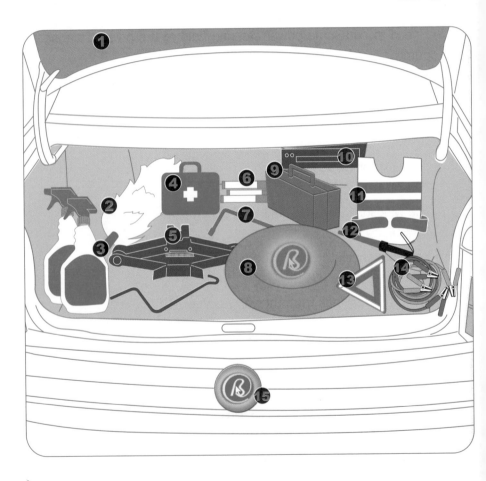

❶ trunk lid [`trʌŋk ˌlɪd] *n.* 後車箱蓋

❷ feather duster [`fɛðɚ ˌdʌstɚ] *n.* 雞毛撢子

❸ cleaning supplies [`klinɪŋ səˌplaɪz] *n.* (複數形) 清潔用品

❹ first aid kit [`fɝst `ed ˌkɪt] *n.* 急救箱

❺ jack [dʒæk] *n.* 千斤頂

❻ flare [flɛr] *n.* 照明彈

❼ lug wrench [`lʌg ˌrɛntʃ] *n.* L 型扳手

❽ spare tire [`spɛr ˌtaɪr] *n.* 備胎

❾ tool kit [`tul ˌkɪt] *n.* 工具箱

❿ CD change [`si `di ˌtʃendʒɚ] *n.* CD 換片箱；CD 換片裝置

⓫ traffic vest [`træfɪk ˌvɛst] *n.* 反光背心

⓬ traffic wand [`træfɪk ˌwɑnd] *n.* 交通指揮棒

⓭ warning triangle [`wɔrnɪŋ `traɪ ˌæŋgl] *n.* 車輛故障標誌

⓮ jumper cable(s) [`dʒʌmpɚ ˌkebl̩ (z)] *n.* 救車線

⓯ emblem [`ɛmbləm] *n.* 標誌

# 06 例句

**運將**

☐ Sorry. I've got a lot of stuff[23] in here. Let me make some room.

抱歉。我這裡面放了很多東西，讓我挪一下空位。

☐ My tail light is burned out.[24] / My bumper is falling off.[25] How embarrassing![26]

我的尾燈燒了。／我的保險桿快掉了。真是不好意思！

☐ I've got a flat[27] tire. Let me get the jack and lug wrench and put on[28] the spare tire.

我的車輪爆胎了。讓我拿一下千斤頂跟 L 型扳手換備胎。

**乘客**

☐ Do you have a first aid kit? I cut myself.

你有急救箱嗎？我割傷自己。

☐ Can I move these cleaning supplies over to make room for my luggage?

我可以把這些清潔用品移過去一點放我的行李嗎？

☐ You forgot to close your fuel door.

你忘了關油箱外蓋。

---

**Word list**

**23** stuff [stʌf] *n.* (不可數) 東西；物品

**24** burn out *phr. v.* 燒壞

**25** fall off *phr. v.* 脫落；掉落

**26** embarrassing [ɪmˋbærəsɪŋ] *adj.* 令人尷尬的

**27** flat [flæt] *adj.* (輪胎) 漏氣的；平的

**28** put on *phr. v.* 換上；穿上

接下來進休息站！

# 4<sup>.2</sup> 運將休息站

這個單元收錄了 **72** 句計程車相關的外國影集引文、**12** 種不同的英文腔調、**12** 項你不知道的台灣資料，還有一篇討論特技駕駛的對話，讓你在排班無聊時消遣一下。

CD2▸34

運將

**A1** Where to, mac?[1] (to a male)[2]

去叨位，老兄？（對男的說）

**A2** Anywhere special, miss?[3] (to a female)[4]

要到什麼特別的地方嗎，小姐？（對女的說）

**A3** Hop[5] in. Take a load off.[6]

跳上來。坐著休息一下。

**A4** What can I do you for?

我能幫你什麼忙？

**A5** At your service.[7] Destination?

全聽你使喚。要上哪？

**A6** Yes, sir? / Yes, ma'am?

是的，先生？／是的，女士？

Word list

**1** mac [mæk] *n.* （口）老兄

**2** male [mel] *n.* 男人／*adj.* 男性的；雄的

**3** miss [mɪs] *n.* 小姐

**4** female [ˋfimel] *n.* 女人／*adj.* 雌的

**5** hop [hɑp] *v.* 跳上；單腳跳

**6** Take a load off. 【俚】坐著休息一下。

**7** at sb's service 提供某人服務；聽從某人的使喚

路邊——經典說法

**乘客**

**B1** Train station. Step on it.[8]
火車站。開快點。

**B2** Anywhere but here. Just drive.
這裡以外，什麼地方都好。開了就對。

**B3** Thanks. Don't mind if I do.
謝啦。我可不介意這麼做。

**B4** Ximending. And don't take the scenic route,[9] pal.[10]
西門町。不要繞路，老兄。

**B5** To the Grand Hotel, if you would.
去圓山大飯店，如果你願意的話。

**B6** The National Theater. I'm in a terrible hurry.
國家戲劇院。我很急。

**Word list**
[8] Step on it. （口）（開）快一點。
[9] scenic route [`sinɪk `rut] *n.* 風景路線
[10] pal [pæl] *n.* （口）朋友；夥伴

CD2►35

 乘客

**A1** OK driver, let's go. (*The Big Sleep*)

好，司機，咱們走吧。（《夜長夢多》）

**A2** Cabbie,[11] I need to get to JFK[12] in 15 minutes—one hundred bucks[13] I make it. (*Taxi*)

運將，我需要在 15 分鐘內抵達甘迺迪國際機場——趕到的話，我給一百美元。（《終極殺陣》）

**A3** (silence) (*Taxi*)

（默不作聲）（《終極殺陣》）

**A4** Hi. 36th and Broadway, Manhattan. Step on it. (*Taxi*)

嗨。曼哈頓，百老匯跟 36 街交叉口。開快點。（《終極殺陣》）

**A5** Follow that car! (*Taxi*)

跟著那輛車！（《終極殺陣》）

**A6** (pompous[14] expression)[15] (*Nick & Jane*)

（不可一世的表情）（《當尼克碰上珍妮》）

---

**Word list**

⓫ cabbie [ˋkæbɪ] *n.* （口）運將 (=cabby)

⓬ JKF 為 John F. Kennedy International Airport 紐約甘迺迪國際機場的簡稱

⓭ buck [bʌk] *n.* 【美】（口）元

⓮ pompous [ˋpɑmpəs] *adj.* 自大的；愛擺架子的

⓯ expression [ɪkˋsprɛʃən] *n.* 表情；臉色

# 02 路邊——電影著名臺詞 I

**B1** OK. (*The Big Sleep*)

好。(《夜長夢多》)

**B2** Done![16] (*Taxi*)

成交!(《終極殺陣》)

**B3** Alright. But I'm still running this meter. (*Taxi*)

好吧!但我還是要跳錶。(《終極殺陣》)

**B4** I don't usually stop for white guys. My way of balancing[17] the universe.[18] (*Taxi*)

我通常是不停車載白人的。這是我平衡這個世界的方式。(《終極殺陣》)

**B5** Buckle up[19] for safety, motherfucker. (*Taxi*)

為了安全,繫上安全帶,X 他媽的。(《終極殺陣》)

**B6** (sniffs)[20] Oh man, what's this? (pull old sandwich from glove box) Sorry lady. (*Nick & Jane*)

(嗅一嗅)噢,天呀,這是什麼?(從前座置物櫃裡拿出一個放了很久的三明治)真歹勢,小姐。(《當尼克碰上珍妮》)

---

**Word list**

16 done [dʌn] *int.* (接受別人開的價碼或提議回答的)成交;好

17 balance [`bæləns] *v.* 使⋯⋯平衡

18 universe [`junə, vɜs] *n.* 全世界;宇宙

19 buckle up *phr. v.* 繫上安全帶

20 sniff [snɪf] *v.* 嗅;聞

CD2▸36

運將

**A1** Sorry, lady. I'm off duty. (*Nick & Jane*)

抱歉，小姐。我休息了。（《當尼克碰上珍妮》）

**A2** You alright? You gonna be OK? (hand woman a tissue)²¹ (*Nick & Jane*)

妳還好吧？妳不會有事吧？（遞給女的一張面紙）（《當尼克碰上珍妮》）

**A3** You want to tell me where you want to go? (*Nick & Jane*)

要不要告訴我妳要去哪裡呢？（《當尼克碰上珍妮》）

**A4** Do you know what the odds²² are of getting the same cab twice in the city? Mmm? Approximately²³ one chance in 96,425.33 reoccurring.²⁴ (*Nick & Jane*)

妳知道在市區裡搭到同一部計程車兩次的機率有多大嗎？嗯？大約 96,425.33 回一次。

**A5** (hit meter) (*Taxi Driver*)

（按錶起跳）（《計程車司機》）

---

**Word list**

㉑ tissue [ˋtɪʃʊ] *n.* 面紙

㉒ odds [ɑdz] *n.* （複數形）機會；可能性

㉓ approximately [əˋprɑksəmɪtly] *adv.* 大概

㉔ reoccur [riəˋkɝ] *v.* 再發生；再出現

# 03 路邊──電影著名臺詞 II

**乘客**

**B1** I just need to get home. (*Nick & Jane*)

我就是得回家。(《當尼克碰上珍妮》)

**B2** (woman crying) Thank you. (*Nick & Jane*)

（女的在哭）謝謝。(《當尼克碰上珍妮》)

**B3** Uh, 79th and Columbus, please. (*Nick & Jane*)

呃，麻煩到哥倫布跟 79 街口。(《當尼克碰上珍妮》)

**B4** Um, this is reminding[25] me a little of Taxi Driver. That was a very scary[26] movie. I think I'm just gonna get another cab. (*Nick & Jane*)

嗯，這有點讓我想到《計程車司機》。那是部非常恐怖的電影。我想我還是搭另一部計程車好了。(《當尼克碰上珍妮》)

**B5** Driver, 48th and 6th, please. (*Taxi Driver*)

司機，麻煩到 48 街和第 6 大道口。(《計程車司機》)

**Word list** [25] remind [rɪ`maɪnd] *v.* 使……想起；提醒
[26] scary [`skɛrɪ] *adj.* 恐怖的

# 04 路邊——電影著名臺詞（下車前）

**CD2▶37**

**乘客**

**A1** If anybody asks you who your fare was tonight, what are going to say? (*Pulp Fiction*)

如果有人問你你今晚的乘客是誰，你會怎麼說？（《黑色追緝令》）

**A2** Here you are, sugar. (hand female cabbie fare) Buy yourself a cigar.[27] (*The Big Sleep*)

來，蜜糖，給妳。（給女運將車資）幫妳自己買根雪茄。（《夜長夢多》）

**A3** Day and night? (*The Big Sleep*)

白天晚上都可以？（《夜長夢多》）

**A4** What do I owe[28] you? (*Nick & Jane*)

我應該給你多少錢？（《當尼克碰上珍妮》）

**A5** Nice talking to you, Travis. (*Taxi Driver*)

很高興跟你說話，崔維斯。（《計程車司機》）

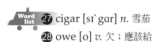

**Word list**

**㉗** cigar [sɪ`gɑr] *n.* 雪茄

**㉘** owe [o] *v.* 欠；應該給

# 04 路邊——電影著名臺詞（下車前）

**B1** Three well-dressed,²⁹ slightly³⁰ toasted³¹ Mexicans. (*Pulp Fiction*)

三個穿著氣派，吸了大麻的墨西哥人。（《黑色追緝令》）

**B2** If you can use me again sometime, call this number. (hand Marlowe card) (*The Big Sleep*)

如果下次你還需要我的話，打這支電話。（給馬洛名片）（《夜長夢多》）

**B3** Uh, night's better. I work during the day. (*The Big Sleep*)

呃，晚上比較好。白天我要工作。（《夜長夢多》）

**B4** The meter's broken. (= you don't need to pay) (*Nick & Jane*)

錶壞了。（＝你不需要付錢）（《當尼克碰上珍妮》）

**B5** Nice talking to you too, sir. You're a good man. (*Taxi Driver*)

我也很高興跟您說話，先生。您是個好人。（《計程車司機》）

Part 4 行進路上

**Word list**
㉙ well-dressed [ˌwɛlˋdrɛst] *adj.* 穿著很體面的
㉚ slightly [ˋslaɪtlɪ] *adv.* 稍微地
㉛ toasted [ˋtostɪd] *adj.* 吸了大麻的；喝醉酒的

CD2 ▸ 38

運將

**A1** Butch.[32] What does it mean?[33] (*Pulp Fiction*)

「布奇」。那是什麼意思？《黑色追緝令》

**A2** Where are we going? (*The Big Sleep*)

我們要去哪？《夜長夢多》

**A3** I'm your girl, bud.[34] (*The Big Sleep*)

我是你的人了，老兄。《夜長夢多》

**A4** I'll take you wherever you want to go. (*Nick & Jane*)

我會載你到任何你想去的地方。《當尼克碰上珍妮》

**A5** (look back at passenger with surprised expression) (*Sex and the City*)

（用吃驚的表情往後看乘客）《慾望城市》

**A6** Take my card in case you ever need some personal car service.[35] (*Nick & Jane*)

拿張我的名片，以便你需要私人包車服務。《當尼克碰上珍妮》

---

**Word list**

㉜ Butch [butʃ] *n.* （口）壯漢；男人婆

㉝ mean [min] *v.* 表示……的意思；意指

㉞ bud [bʌd] *n.* （口）老兄 (=buddy [ˋbʌdɪ])

㉟ personal car service [ˋpɝsn̩ ˋkɑr ˏsɝvɪs] *n.* 私人包車服務；私人座車服務

# 05 車上——電影／影集著名臺詞Ⅰ

乘客

**B1** I'm an American, honey. Our names don't mean shit. (*Pulp Fiction*)

親愛的，我是個美國人。我們的名字沒啥屁意思。（《黑色追緝令》）

**B2** Around the corner, then take it easy. Follow a car—tail[36] job. (*The Big Sleep*)

轉過街角，然後慢慢開。跟一輛車——跟監工作。（《夜長夢多》）

**B3** That station wagon[37] coming out of the alley, that's the one. (*The Big Sleep*)

那輛從巷子出來的旅行車，就是那輛。（《夜長夢多》）

**B4** I've never been in the front seat of a cab before. Big windshield. (*Nick & Jane*)

我以前從來沒坐過計程車的前座。擋風玻璃好大。（《當尼克碰上珍妮》）

**B5** Hello! You're driving! (*Sex and the City*)

哈囉！你現在在開車耶！（《慾望城市》）

**B6** Thank you. I will. (*Nick & Jane*)

謝謝，我會的。（《當尼克碰上珍妮》）

 **36** tail [tel] *n.* 跟監者；尾部／*v.* 盯梢

**37** station wagon [ˋsteʃən͵wægən] *n.* 旅行車（型似轎車，後車箱空間加大）

CD2 ▸▸ 39

**運將先說**

**A1** Where you from? (*The Terminal*)

你哪來的？（《航站情緣》）

**A2** Hey ... what do you call the middle of a song? (*Who Framed Roger Rabbit*)

嘿……，一首歌的中間叫什麼？（《威探闖通關》）

**A3** First time in LA?[38] (*Collateral*)

第一次到洛杉磯？（《落日殺神》）

**運將回答**

**A4** Umm, Thursday! (*The Terminal*)

嗯，星期四！（《航站情緣》）

**A5** He wants to know if you'll marry him. (*Men of Honor*)

他想知道妳是否願意嫁給他。（《怒海潛降》）

**A6** Yeah, I share[39] it with the day-shift[40] guy. (*Collateral*)

對呀，我跟白天班的傢伙輪流開。（《落日殺神》）

**A7** I know the cops are on our tail. What do you think I am? Blind?[41] (*Who Framed Roger Rabbit*)

我知道條子在我們後面。你以為我是什麼？瞎子嗎？

---

**Word list**

38 LA 為 Los Angeles [los `ændʒələs] *n.* 【美】洛杉磯的縮寫

39 share [ʃɛr] *v.* 共同使用；分享

40 shift [ʃɪft] *n.* 輪班（day-shift [`de,ʃɪft] *n.* 日班）

41 blind [blaɪnd] *adj.* 盲的

# 06 車上——電影／影集著名臺詞 II

乘客回答

**B1** Krakozhia. I'm Victor Navorski. (*The Terminal*)

夸科夏共和國。我叫威特·賴瓦斯基。（《航站情緣》）

**B2** A bridge. (*Who Framed Roger Rabbit*)

中段。（《威探闖通關》）

**B3** No. Tell you the truth. Whenever I'm here, I can't wait to leave. Too sprawled out.[42] (*Collateral*)

不是。老實跟你說，我每次來這裡，都迫不及待想離開。太擴散了。（《落日殺神》）

乘客先說

**B4** When do you come to New York? (*The Terminal*)

你什麼時候來紐約的？（《航站情緣》）

**B5** (Jo looks back and sees Carl running after the cab) What? (*Men of Honor*)

（喬往後看，看到卡爾追著計程車跑）什麼？（《怒海潛降》）

**B6** This is the cleanest cab I've been in. Regular[43] ride? (*Collateral*)

這是我坐過最乾淨的計程車了。你固定開這部嗎？（《落日殺神》）

**B7** The cops are still on our tail! (*Who Framed Roger Rabbit*)

條子還是跟在我們後面！（《威探闖通關》）

---

**Word list** 42 sprawl out *phr. v.* 手腳放鬆地向外伸展開；都市不規則地擴張、延伸

43 regular [ˋrɛgjələ] *adj.* 經常的；定時的

Part 4 行進路上

CD2▸**40**

台北。新生南路跟長安東路口。

☐ Taipei. Hsinsheng S. Road and Chang'an E. Road.
(can speak Chinese) 洋涇濱英文
☐ Taipei. Hsinsheng S. Road and Chang'an E. Road.
(North American) 北美腔
☐ Taipei. Hsinsheng S. Road and Chang'an E. Road.
(Australian) 澳洲腔
☐ Taipei. Hsinsheng S. Road and Chang'an E. Road.
(UK) 英國腔
☐ Taipei. Hsinsheng S. Road and Chang'an E. Road.
(Pilipino) 菲律賓腔
☐ Taipei. Hsinsheng S. Road and Chang'an E. Road.
(Japanese) 日本腔

- [ ] Taipei. Hsinsheng S. Road and Chang'an E. Road. (African) 非洲腔
- [ ] Taipei. Hsinsheng S. Road and Chang'an E. Road. (Middle Eastern) 中東腔
- [ ] Taipei. Hsinsheng S. Road and Chang'an E. Road. (South American) 南美腔
- [ ] Taipei. Hsinsheng S. Road and Chang'an E. Road. (German) 德國腔
- [ ] Taipei. Hsinsheng S. Road and Chang'an E. Road. (had a tooth pulled) 有顆牙被拔
- [ ] Taipei. Hsinsheng S. Road and Chang'an E. Road. (drunk) 喝醉酒

CD2 ▸ 41

☐ In May 2006, 64% of all email spam[44] was sent from Taiwan.
2006 年 5 月時，有 **64%** 的電子垃圾郵件是從台灣寄出的。

☐ There are about 23 million people on this island. About the same population[45] as Canada.
大約有兩千三百萬人住在這個小島上，差不多等於加拿大的人口。

☐ Taiwan has three nuclear[46] power plants but 75% of the electricity[47] comes from coal[48] and hydroelectric[49] power.
台灣有三座核能發電廠，但 **75%** 的電力是靠煤和水力發電產生的。

☐ The navy[50] has four Kidd class destroyers.[51] They cost over 730 million US dollars (US$730,000,000).
中華民國海軍擁有四艘紀德級驅逐艦。它們價值超過七億三千萬美元 (US$730,000,000)。

☐ Two thousand four hundred (2,400) people died[52] in the nine twenty-one (921) earthquake.[53]
九二一 **(921)** 大地震有兩千四百個人 **(2,400)** 死亡。

---

**Word list**

**44** spam [spæm] *n.*【電腦】垃圾郵件

**45** population [ˌpɑpjəˋleʃən] *n.* 人口

**46** nuclear power plant [ˋnjuklɪə ˋpauə ˌplænt] *n.* 核能發電廠

**47** electricity [ˌɪlɛkˋtrɪsətɪ] *n.* 電力；電

**48** coal [kol] *n.* 煤

**49** hydroelectric [ˌhaɪdroɪˋlɛktrɪk] *adj.* 水力發電的

**50** navy [ˋnevɪ] *n.* 海軍

**51** destroyer [dɪˋstrɔɪə] *n.* 驅逐艦

**52** die [daɪ] *v.* 死

**53** earthquake [ˋɝθˌkwek] *n.* 地震

☐ This is the only place in the world with betel nut beauties.
全世界只有這個地方有檳榔西施。

☐ Most of the Chinese content[54] on Wikipedia[55] comes from Taiwanese writers.
維基百科上大部分的中文內容是台灣人寫的。

☐ The same company that owns 7-Eleven operates[56] Starbucks.
擁有統一超商的公司也是星巴克的經營者。

☐ The biggest semiconductor[57] factory in the world is here.
全球最大的半導體工廠在這裡。

☐ The world's tallest building is in Taipei. But you knew that.
全球最高的建築物在台北，但這個你知道。

☐ Over half of China's high-tech[58] exports[59] are made in Taiwanese-owned factories.
中國大陸有一半以上的高科技輸出品是由台商工廠製造的。

☐ You can pay most of your bills[60] in convenience stores[61]—there are over 4,200 7-Elevens here. (As of August 27, 2006: 4,273)
你大部分的帳單都能在便利商店繳款——這裡有超過 4,200 間的統一超商。
（2006 年 08 月 27 日的店數總計為 4,273 間）

**Word list**

54 content [`kɑntɛnt] n. 內容
55 Wikipedia [ˌwɪkə`pidɪə] 維基百科，一部可查可寫的多語網路百科全書，網址為 www.wikipedia.org
56 operate [`ɑpəˌret] v. 經營；運作
57 semiconductor [ˌsɛmɪkən`dʌktə] n. 【電】半導體
58 high-tech [`haɪ`tɛk] adj. 高科技的
59 export [`ɛksport] n. 輸出品；出口
60 bill [bɪl] n. 帳單
61 convenience store [kən`vinjəns ˌstor] n. 便利商店

## 09 討論特技駕駛——運將

☐ I used to be a stunt[62] driver in Hong Kong.[63]
我在香港曾經是個特技駕駛。

☐ I feel like doing some donuts.[64] Hold on!
我想來幾圈 360° 原地迴轉。抓緊！

☐ I know how to drive my car up on two wheels.
我知道怎麼傾斜車身用側雙輪開車。

☐ Let's see if I can do a second gear scratch.[65]
咱們來看我是不是能換二檔軋出聲音。

☐ I took my car off[66] a cool jump yesterday.
昨天我讓整台車很帥地飛跳起來。

☐ Sorry. I got sideways[67] around that turn[68] back there.
抱歉，剛才轉彎那裡我甩尾了。

---

**Word list**

62 stunt [stʌnt] *n.* 特技表演

63 Hong Kong [ˋhɑŋ ˋkɑŋ] *n.* 香港（常縮寫為 HK）

64 do donuts [ˋdonəts] (=do doughnuts) 讓車子 360° 原地轉圈

65 scratch [skrætʃ] *n.* 括擦聲；刮痕

66 take sth. off 使某物脫離地面

67 sideways [ˋsaɪd‚wez] *adj.* 斜向一邊的／*adv.* 斜向一邊地

68 turn [tɜn] *n.* 轉角；轉彎處

# 10 討論特技駕駛——乘客

☐ Hey. See if you can catch some air (off that bump).[69]

嘿，看你是不是能飛過去（那個地面凸起物）。

☐ Why don't you try to peel out?[70]

你何不試試原地加速急衝？

☐ Do you know how to do a Rockford?[71]

你知道怎麼倒車迴轉 180° 往前開嗎？

☐ Bump that car and make it spin out.

撞那台車，讓它旋轉出去。

☐ Drifting[72] looks pretty fun. Can you do it?

甩尾看起來蠻好玩的。你會不會？

☐ Do a 180! That'll ditch[73] the car behind us!

來個 180° 迴轉！那樣就能甩掉我們後面那台車！

Part
4
行
進
路
上

**69** bump [bʌmp] *n.* （路面等的）凸塊／*v.* 撞；碰

**70** peel out *phr. v.* 加速讓車子嘰嘰作響急衝出去

**71** Rockford [`rɑk͵fəd] 由美國電視影集 *The Rockford Files* 的男主角 Jim Rockford 而來，他在影集裡表演倒車迴旋 180° 後往前繼續開聞名

**72** drifting [`drɪftɪŋ] *n.* 甩尾；漂移

**73** ditch [dɪtʃ] *v.* （口）甩掉；拋棄

國家圖書館出版品預行編目資料

計程車 900 句典 / Brian Greene 作. --初版.
--臺北市；貝塔，
2006〔民 95〕 面： 公分
參考書目：面

ISBN 978-957-729-607-8（平裝附光碟片）

1. 英國語言—會話

805.188 95016816

# 計程車 900 句典
*Overheard in a Taxi*

作　　者／Brian Greene
總 編 審／王復國
執行編輯／邱慧菁

出　　版／貝塔出版有限公司
地　　址／100 台北市館前路 12 號 11 樓
電　　話／(02)2314-2525
傳　　真／(02)2312-3535
郵　　撥／19493777 貝塔出版有限公司
客服專線／(02)2314-3535
客服信箱／btservice@betamedia.com.tw

總 經 銷／時報文化出版企業股份有限公司
地　　址／桃園市龜山區萬壽路二段 351 號
電　　話／(02) 2306-6842

出版日期／2017 年 10 月初版三刷
定　　價／250 元
ISBN-10 ： 957-729-607-6
ISBN-13 ： 978-957-729-607-8

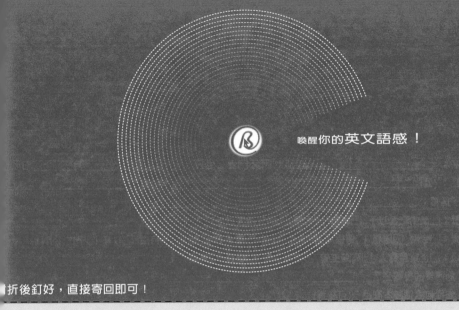

喚醒你的英文語感！

折後釘好，直接寄回即可！

100 台北市中正區館前路12號11樓

 貝塔語言出版　收
Beta Multimedia Publishing

 寄件者住址 ☐☐☐

讀者服務專線（02）2314-3535　讀者服務傳真（02）2312-3535
客戶服務信箱　btservice@betamedia.com.tw

**www.betamedia.com.tw**

謝謝您購買本書！！

貝塔語言擁有最優良之英文學習書籍，為提供您最佳的英語學習資訊，您填妥此表後寄回（免貼郵票）將可不定期免費收到本公司最新發行書訊及活動訊息！

姓名：_____　性別：□男 □女　生日：_____年_____月_____日

電話：(公)_____(宅)_____(手機)_____

電子信箱：_____

學歷：□高中職含以下 □專科 □大學 □研究所含以上

職業：□金融 □服務 □傳播 □製造 □資訊 □軍公教 □出版 □自由 □教育 □學生 □其他

職級：□企業負責人 □高階主管 □中階主管 □職員 □專業人士

1. 您購買的書籍是？_____

2. 您從何處得知本產品？(可複選)

　　□書店 □網路 □書展 □校園活動 □廣告信函 □他人推薦 □新聞報導 □其他

3. 您覺得本產品價格：

　　□偏高 □合理 □偏低

4. 請問目前您每週花了多少時間學英語？

　　□不到十分鐘 □十分鐘以上，但不到半小時 □半小時以上，但不到一小時

　　□一小時以上，但不到兩小時 □兩個小時以上 □ 不一定

5. 通常在選擇語言學習書時，哪些因素是您會考慮的？

　　□ 封面 □內容、實用性 □品牌 □媒體、朋友推薦 □價格 □其他_____

6. 市面上您最需要的語言書種類為？

　　□聽力 □閱讀 □文法 □口說 □寫作 □其他_____

7. 通常您會透過何種方式選購語言學習書籍？

　　□書店門市 □網路書店 □郵購 □直接找出版社 □學校或公司團購

　　□其他_____

8. 給我們的建議：_____

_____

喚醒你的英文語感！

Get a Feel for English !